FLOWER OF HEAVEN

A Novel

JULIEN AYOTTE

This is a work of fiction. Names, characters, places and incidents are the products of the author's imagination or are used fictionally. Any resemblance to actual events, locales or persons, living or dead, is entirely coincidental.

Author Photo Credit: Glenn Ruga

ISBN: 1479274739

ISBN 13: 9781479274734

Library of Congress Control Number: 2012916918
CreateSpace Independent Publishing Platform
North Charleston, South Carolina

To my wife, Pauline, and my children,
Barbara, David, and Julie, with love

CHAPTER 1

What is it about New England that the natives find so appealing? Jim Howard asked himself every so often while never once giving a thought to moving away from this most confusing of climates in the world. As an insurance salesman in a small city of seventy-five thousand people in the northern corner of Rhode Island, Jim was constantly on the road to surrounding communities drumming up as many new customers as he could from his company's weekly ad in the *Providence Sunday Journal.*

What is it, he pondered that November day in 1987, keeping New Englanders satisfied, in spite of the upcoming below-zero temperatures for the next three or four months, not to mention the ridiculous fuel bills that go along with it. From conversations he had with most of his prospective customers, none of them either liked the cold or were anxious for it to come, and yet, they would never dream of leaving it. Oh sure, they'd talk about retiring South and how they couldn't wait, but Jim knew this was typical New Englander talk, never once really expecting to shed this climate.

"Fr. Richard Merrill, St. Matthew's Rectory, 310 Mendon Road, Lincoln, RI," read the returned post card from last week's ad. "What the hell does a priest want with life insurance?" he mumbled to himself, obviously expecting his trip to the nearby town to be another waste of time or, at best, the sale of a cheap term policy which didn't generate much in the way of renewed commissions each year from the policy premiums. Who would he name as the beneficiary? Why waste his money on insurance? Insurance is for protection, he thought, and to prevent financial hardship on a family because of the loss of a loved one. He had never sold a policy to a priest before. What would he say, "Father, how many children do you have?" or "we've got to consider the blackout years, Father, those years where you could be unemployed or disabled until you're eligible for Social Security benefit."

Continental Life in Providence, where Jim's home office was located, and Harry Abramian, Jim's regional manager, didn't care who the post card came from. It was from an interested potential client that required follow-up and the inquirer was located in Jim's territory. Normally, Jim would have chucked the reply in the trash can and merely reported to Harry that Father Merrill changed his mind and had no further interest. Jim's curiosity, if for no other reason, made him call Father Merrill that Thursday afternoon to set up an appointment to discuss exactly what he had in mind. They agreed to meet the next day.

"Good afternoon, St. Matthew's, may I help you?" a cheery little voice echoed with a slight Irish accent.

"Father Merrill, please, Jim Howard from Continental Life calling."

The housekeeper at the rectory door warmly invited him in. "Please be kind enough to have a seat in the living room, and I'll get Father Dick for you."

Jim, a Roman Catholic himself, could easily relate to being inside a rectory, the home and business offices, all in one, for Catholic priests. He was very active in his parish's activities and had, on more than one occasion, attended various functions in the same setting. As he sat in the parlor, he couldn't help but notice the plush décor of the room. Every piece of furniture perfectly placed where you'd expect it; rich furniture typical of the inside of rectories where money is no object. Image is all that counts. After all, he thought, every parish pastor will tell you how important it is for the religious to have proper quarters to show off to parishioners and to the bishop when he visits. Oddly enough though, as he recalled, the bishop probably visits each parish but once a year and Jim couldn't help but notice that these furnishings were very expensive looking, not typical of the homes within the community it served.

Why is it that people who do not pay for what they have always want and expect the best? All that ran through his mind was the thought of a domineering Father Merrill, the "I deserve the best" type who had a few bucks to his name and figured life insurance as an investment even if he didn't need it. A typical priest who complains about his schedule and the number of Masses he has to say each week, not to mention the funerals, weddings, and other activities he's involved in. Don't forget the sermon he must prepare for each week, a chore that priests would have you believe is like preparing for a weekly inaugural address.

"Mr. Howard, Father Dick Merrill." Jim startled as a huge man approached him and introduced himself. This was no ordinary looking priest, six feet, four inches tall, silver white hair, very tanned, and a smile that had pain written all over it.

"Nice to meet you, Father. Beautiful rectory you've got here."

Father Dick's eyes quickly scanned the room as if he hadn't even noticed where he was. He appeared to be out of place with the richness of it all, as if he would have felt more at ease in a mission on a tropical island with a grass hut for a church and a hammock for a rectory. Maybe it was the sandals he was wearing and the big straw hat he had just removed as he entered the room.

"I hate this weather, would have stayed where I was, where it's warm. I'm getting too old for cold weather and it's not even winter yet!" Father Dick motioned to Jim to sit down as he sat facing him. "You're a man who's been recommended to me because of your honesty, loyalty, courage, and sincerity in your work and in your whole life, Mr. Howard."

"Excuse me, Father," Jim chimed in. "I represent an insurance company, but something tells me this isn't about life insurance."

"Harry Abramian sent you to see me only because I asked him to; the post card was just a way to get you here. Actually, Mr. Howard, I used Mr. Abramian as a way to get you but your name was really given to me by Jack Bumpus, you probably remember him as Major Jack Bumpus, your old military boss some years ago."

"Excuse me for asking, Father," blurted out the more than startled Jim Howard. "How in the world do you know Jack Bumpus? He doesn't exactly hang out in your circle of people."

It was obvious to Father Dick by now that Jim Howard's curiosity had reached a level of excitement and that he suspected there was going to be more to this little afternoon meeting than the sale of a small life insurance policy to a local parish priest.

"Please, Mr. Howard, let me explain", said Father Dick in an attempt to bring the conversation down to an easy pace again. "Jack and I met in 1975 in Haiti. I was visiting some missionary friends of mine there as I do, normally about once a year, when I take my vacation from parish work. One afternoon during one of my shopping trips to Port-au-Prince, a car nearly hit me when I was crossing one of the streets in the city. Actually, I fell to the pavement to avoid the oncoming car."

"There I am, sprawled out on the ground in tourist clothes, wearing a straw hat, and native Haitians going about their business as if I wasn't even there. Then a hand was extended to help me up and Jack Bumpus was on the other end of the hand. There he was, smiling from ear to ear, and simply said, "You gotta be a tourist. Nobody else comes within ten feet of the maniacs driving on these streets."

As he continued to speak, Father Dick saw that Jim Howard's interest was becoming more intense in what surely, to Jim, was a name from the past, a past he had hoped to forget about and hadn't thought of for nearly ten years.

Father Dick had merely introduced himself as Dick Merrill when he thanked the man who had come to his assistance, the man with the big smile and rugged face that appeared to have a thousand stories behind it. It was quite customary, Father Dick recalled, not to make a big deal of being a priest when vacationing, and he didn't like the people he met feeling as if they had to always watch what they said because they knew he was a priest.

Dick Merrill and Jack Bumpus hit it off from the very start, as if Jack Bumpus had adopted this hopeless tourist with the huge frame but gentle manner. There was something about Dick Merrill that Bumpus liked, his sincere appreciation for the helping hand, his offer to buy him a drink, which Jack never refused, or the instant reaction some people get at meeting fellow Americans in foreign surroundings. As often as Father Dick had been to Haiti, he would still fumble his way around the streets of the cities. This was his fifth visit to his old seminarian buddy, Father Edward McNeil, who had left his parish in Racine, Wisconsin, in 1969 to help the poor in Haiti.

After exchanging small talk about the weather and other general conditions in Port-au-Prince, Jack asked Father Dick what he was doing in Haiti, explaining in no uncertain terms that the country wasn't exactly a garden spot for tourism, nor was it safe for a foreigner to walk the streets. Jack pointed out to Father Dick that he stood out like a bull in the arena, a prime target for pickpockets, muggers, beggars, you name it.

"I could say the same for you, you know," exclaimed Father Dick, trying not look as awkward as he knew he really was in this situation.

"It's different for me, Dick; I'm used to this crap and the natives know it," chuckled Jack, obviously pleased at the way Father Dick was attempting to protect his ego.

"I'm what you would call a soldier of fortune, a mercenary, a military man who's been trained to expect the worst and then to cope with it under most circumstances. I just finished an assignment for my employer over here and I'll be heading back to the States in a couple of days. What brings you to this god-forsaken place?"

When Father Dick revealed that he was a priest, Jack was surprised and excited, not so much at learning that this new acquaintance was a man of the cloth, but rather at the prospect that Father Dick knew his way around more than he originally thought.

Father Dick somehow felt he had to tell Jack Bumpus who he really was and, casual outfit or not, related to him how he was visiting his missionary friend assigned to a small village on the coast.

Jack Bumpus was not a popular person to be roaming around the city. Local military authorities somehow knew of his clandestine activities and were watching him like a hawk everywhere he went. Even at his hotel, Jack did not feel safe sleeping behind locked doors.

"You wouldn't have a room to spare at the mission until my flight to the States in a couple of days, would you, Dick, or should I call you Father Merrill?" Jack asked. "I'd really like to get a good night's rest without keeping an eye and ear open at the hotel. I'll pay you or your missionary friend for the room and I'll even throw in a hundred dollars for food and drink for the next two days."

Father Dick quickly accepted the offer, knowing that Father McNeil would be ecstatic at the money for the mission, and both of them headed to pick up Jack's luggage and check out of the hotel. To avoid much attention, Jack gave money to Father Dick to cover the hotel bill while

Jack left using the rear entrance after picking up his bags. Once Father Dick had settled the hotel bill at the front desk, he met Jack at the bus depot, two streets over, and they boarded the next bus headed for the trip back to Saint Marc, a small town where the mission was located.

Mercenaries, Father Dick reflected as the bus bounced along the dirt road, are hired guns, not so much for good causes but, oftentimes to the highest bidder. What kind of person could Jack Bumpus be to sell himself to any government or rebel group making attempts to gain control of some underdeveloped country? Who was this man who sat next to him on the bus, where did he come from and why would he so easily admit to a stranger that he's a mercenary? And yet, he was friendly and generous and American, a welcome relief to Father Dick in a country where Americans were scarce except at missions outside the main cities, missions like the one outside of Saint Marc. Bumpus' charismatic approach puzzled Father Dick and he wasn't sure that this generous man did not have more in mind than just a place to stay for a few days. No one offers that much money for a room, sight unseen, unless perhaps he himself wanted to remain unseen.

Father Dick seemed to want to overlook Jack Bumpus' way of life in exchange for non-religious companionship, if only for a day or two. After all, he thought, this is supposed to be a vacation. And besides, pondered Father Dick, he would surely get a chance to know this man better in the next two days, so why prejudge him before he had his say. Priests were trained to be good listeners and Jack appeared, to Father Dick, to be an extrovert, very outspoken and likely to reveal himself at some point before his flight left Haiti.

At 3:00 p.m. the bus approached the outskirts of the town and stopped at the entrance to the mission compound. When Jack first laid eyes on the mission area, he probably thought about going back to Port-au-Prince and taking his chances at the hotel. Father Dick had told him that the facilities were primitive but that the mission was a paradise when compared to the native conditions in the area. But Jack had seen worse, Father Dick was certain, as the bus stopped to let them out.

Beyond the large wooden structure, similar to Army barracks, both men could see children gathered together listening to a white-haired, very tanned priest dressed in a long white robe.

"Father McNeil, I'd like you to meet Jack Bumpus. I met him in the city and he was helpful to me after I nearly was hit by a car," shouted Father Dick. He shouted because Father McNeil was hard of hearing and hearing aids cost money, money that could be used to buy more food, clothing and tools for the local residents in need.

"Nice to meet you, Mr. Bumpus. Anyone who helps out a friend of mine is welcome here anytime. Are you hurt, Dicky?" asked Father McNeil with genuine concern for his friend's well-being.

"No, no, I'm fine, Eddie, more embarrassed than anything. Jack wants to stay with us for a couple of days before his flight back to the States, if that's okay with you? He's even offered to pay a hundred dollars to the mission to help out."

"One hundred dollars? Do you know what that kind of money can do over here?" gleamed Father McNeil, a man in his mid-fifties, whose years in the hot sun had added too many wrinkles to his appearance. "Let's go inside to the kitchen and have some iced tea. I also have some wine and brandy if you'd rather have that," motioned Father McNeil as they headed for the priest's quarters in a small building adjacent to the wooden one.

The mission was small, three buildings in all, but it was clean. The left side of the main building served as a local clinic and was run by three nuns from the Presentation of Mary order. No major ailments were treated there but it took care of emergencies and infections that set in from time to time; and besides, it was free. The right side of the building was a chapel and part-time school during the day. Adjacent to the building, on each side, were two old Quonset huts, each with screened-in porches added to the front. One was used to house the nuns and to store food and supplies received from the States for distribution to the people in the district. The other was Father McNeil's house and the kitchen for feeding needy people at evening meals. It was furnished with wooden tables and benches, assorted chairs, and counters where food was served cafeteria style. Electricity was restricted to a few overhead lighting fixtures and several extension cords connected to one or two outlets against a wall.

"Not the greatest accommodations for you, Mr. Bumpus, but we're not here for a vacation or to live in luxury," Father McNeil said as the three walked through the open kitchen area to reach the living quarters at the rear of the building. "We're lucky, though. We've got some electricity and I've got a generator out back when the electricity goes out more often than not. That's more than the other two missions on the island have; so, I'm more fortunate than they are."

"What'll it be folks, iced tea or spirits?" Jack Bumpus passed on the tea and settled for a brandy while the two others had iced tea. After several minutes of assurance that Father Dick was not hurt in any way, Father McNeil turned his attention to Jack Bumpus. "We don't get too many visitors here, Mister Bumpus, except for fellow priests who spend a week or so down here to get a break from their rich parishes up North," Father McNeil stated with curiosity in his voice. "What brings you to this tropical paradise you see before you?"

"I'm a representative from a textile manufacturer in North Carolina who's been thinking of opening a plant in Haiti, Father, and I just came down to explore the possibilities. I've been meeting with local officials in Port-au-Prince."

Father Dick's face turned pale in amazement and he immediately turned away from Jack Bumpus and stood up to face Father McNeil. "Eddie, why don't I show Jack where he's going to sleep and he can put his luggage there and freshen up before we get ready for dinner."

"Great idea, Dick," chimed Father McNeil. "I've got to get back to the children anyway for a while, and then I want to check in on the clinic and see how the sisters are doing." The nuns who prepared enough food for about two hundred people served dinner nightly at 7:00 p.m. Meals consisted mostly of the basic staples, rice and vegetables, the rice coming from supplies from the States and the vegetables, for the most part, grown in the fields nearby. Father McNeil was proud of what the mission had accomplished with the agricultural tools they had, allowing the natives to grow their own food and even selling some of it to hotels and restaurants in the city.

To allow time for meal preparation, the clinic closed at 4:00 p.m., enough time for the sisters to rest before beginning the chores to get dinner ready. "We'll talk some more at dinner, Mr. Bumpus," shouted Father McNeil as he headed out the kitchen.

Father Dick, however, was not finished with Jack Bumpus.

CHAPTER 2

"Is there some explanation you'd care to share with me, Jack, on that little speech you just gave Father McNeil?" Father Dick posed with a very stern look of disgust on his face. "I don't really know who you are and I get the distinct feeling that what you're about to tell me isn't going to help me know you any better."

"Trust me, Dick," echoed Jack, "I'll tell you more later but not in front of Father McNeil. I'll explain it to you tonight but I'd like to check this place out and, maybe, talk to the locals first." With that, Jack got up from his chair and waited, with luggage in hand, for Father Dick to lead the way.

Jack could obviously see doubt written all over Father Dick's face as they entered the bedroom area of the priest's quarters. Father Dick was silent through this brief period other than to point the room out to Jack, an eight-by-ten-foot partitioned area next to his own similar room opposite Father McNeil's slightly larger area. The room was plain: a twin bed, a bureau, a chair under a small-screened window and a table to be used as a closet or nightstand.

* * *

"That's Jack, alright, biggest bullshit artist I've ever met," Jim Howard blurted, as if somewhat disgusted and partly with a smile on his face. "I can imagine how he tried to talk his way out of that one with you, Father," Jim continued, "but, what does a visit to Haiti, ten years ago, and Jack Bumpus have to do with me?"

"I'm getting to that, bear with me," pleaded Father Dick who, by now, was trying to speed up the story to make his point before Jim Howard had a chance to get too uneasy about the whole conversation. The housekeeper appeared at the parlor door with a tray of cookies and a pot of fresh coffee, which she merely placed on a coffee table between Jim and Father Dick and quietly left the room, sliding the divider doors closed behind her as she left.

* * *

"I'm in trouble, Dick," Jack Bumpus had told Father Dick. "Our group had to leave Cuba in a hurry three days ago and the Cuban authorities tracked us to Haiti. My other associates and I decided to split up and go it alone; we figured we had a better shot at making it back to the States alone and we wouldn't draw as much attention from the local authorities that way. The Cubans merely buy off the locals here for information, and they'd turn their own mothers over to them for the right price."

"I don't have a passport, so I've got to lay low for a couple of days to try to figure out what I'm going to do. I'll stay out of your hair and you won't even know I'm here, Dick, just play along with me on this with Father McNeil. You're a tourist and you'll be out of Haiti in a couple of days yourself. Father McNeil lives here. If they find out I stayed here and he knew what I did for a living, they'd get it out of him. This way, all he knows is that I'm a guy working for a textile company here on a business trip."

Father Dick was angry, his face and neck were as red as they could be, and it took all he had not to jump up and scream at this man who had used him and had now jeopardized what his long-time friend had worked for in Haiti for years by harboring a man wanted by the authorities without even knowing it.

"I do what I have to in my business, Dick, sometimes I hurt people I don't mean to, but I always try to even it out, even if it takes me a long time to do it; I make it up to people who get caught up in my world, even when they don't ask for it," said Jack, almost apologizing for what he'd already done but, somehow in the same breath, implying that he'd do it again if he had to.

"I expect you gone from here, Mr. Bumpus," Father Dick emphasized using the formality of his sudden terminated relationship with his new acquaintance, "and the sooner, the better. Father McNeil may begin to like you and I don't think I want that to happen."

"Dick, come quick, I need your help!" Father Dick could hear from outside the bedroom. As he headed through the kitchen area, there was a frantic Father

McNeil, rushing in to announce an outbreak of fever at a nearby village. He had to leave at once with one of the nuns from the clinic to attend to the sick. Father Dick offered to go with him and, while they both gathered a few things needed for the short trip, Jack Bumpus asked if there was anything he could do to help.

"No, no, Mr. Bumpus, your kindness for the mission is more than enough. We should be back in a day or so. In the meantime, please make yourself as comfortable as possible. My house is your house," uttered Father McNeil as he hurried out the door with Father Dick at his heels. The last glimpse from Father Dick toward Jack Bumpus was self-explanatory.

"Indeed, Mr. Bumpus, you've done enough."

Two days later, the priests returned to the mission, both exhausted yet relieved that the fever in the village was under control. As a precaution, Father McNeil had asked a nun to stay behind for a few more days to tend to any new cases that might emerge. Medical supplies were adequate to handle this type of fever, common in countries with tropical climates and symptomatic of malaria, although curable with proper treatment and injections.

As he had wished, Father Dick had a letter waiting for him from Jack Bumpus, who was nowhere to be found. According to one of the nuns at the clinic, Jack had left the following morning after the two priests had departed for the stricken village. "Dear Dick," the note read, "Sorry for the trouble I may have caused you and Father McNeil. Wish I could stay to explain more but I just thought of a way to get off this island and I can't pass it up. I got your address from your luggage tags and I'll contact you soon, if all goes well." The note was simply signed Jack and was followed by a postscript, "The $100 is for the mission as I promised. Please destroy this note after you've read it."

For the remainder of the week, there was little other excitement at the mission and, as Father Dick relaxed on the screened-in porch one evening, he couldn't help but think about the strange incident with Jack Bumpus just several days earlier. It would have been nice to know more about this man who was out of Father Dick's life almost as quickly as he had entered it.

"Better get packed before you turn in, Dick," said Father McNeil as he joined Father Dick with a glass of brandy in each hand. "I've got to take you to the airport early tomorrow. You know how bad the travel schedules are at the airport, as much as I'd love for you to stay longer. If you should hear from Mr. Bumpus when you get back, do me a favor and send me his address, will you? I'd like to thank him for his donation to the mission, and he didn't even stay more than one night. Nice fellow that Mr. Bumpus."

The next evening Father Dick was back in New England and at St. Matthew's. He had the unusual feeling during the return flight home that he would hear from Jack Bumpus again. Whether he wanted to or not, he really wasn't sure.

* * *

"I heard from Jack Bumpus three weeks after my return from Haiti," Father Dick related to Jim who, by now, was content in sitting back and listening to this account involving an old comrade.

Father Dick had received a letter from Bumpus with a passport included; Father McNeil's passport. Jack had apparently removed Father McNeil's picture from the passport and had replaced it with his own, dressed in a priest's black suit. As the letter continued, Father McNeil's black suit had been damaged by Bumpus accidentally and was in no condition to be returned. Enclosed was $200 in cash to cover the cost of replacing the suit. He asked Father Dick to mail the passport to Father McNeil with the money and to offer his apologies the best way he saw fit.

The letter was postmarked from San Diego with a post office box number only. Jack Bumpus closed by telling Father Dick that if he could repay the favor someday, he would.

* * *

"That's how I know Jack Bumpus, Mr. Howard," said Father Dick, "and now, ten years later, I needed a favor and I wrote to the same box number and he gave me your name. He really thinks highly of you, Mr. Howard. Were the two of you close in your military days?"

"Close? Nobody got too close to Jack, Father," said Jim shaking his head. "Jack believed that if you didn't get too close to somebody in combat, you wouldn't become emotional if something happened to one of your men. He was strictly by the book. A job had to be done and he wouldn't let any personal feelings sway his decision when he had to send guys out on a mission back in 'Nam."

"Then why did he recommend that I contact you?" Father Dick questioned.

"Because he saved my skin over there and he knows that I owe him my life, that's why," Jim countered. "The fact that I can speak five languages, spent my early Army career in the Military Police and a couple of years as a private investigator before this job, I'm sure that's all got a lot to do with it also, Father, whatever it is you're looking for."

Jim recollected how the two men had been on a patrol one day in the delta. Major Bumpus made it a practice of moving his men slowly and cautiously when on missions in the jungle area. He knew all too well the booby traps and primitive weaponry used by the Vietcong. Jack had been one of the few officers who had signed on for a second tour of duty in Vietnam. A rare breed, a man more interested in what he was fighting for than most others assigned to him, but Jack was about to make a mistake. He was about to get involved with one of his men. It's not the kind of thing you can get ready for, it sort of just happens and you have to address it at the moment as best you can.

No Vietcong had been sighted that day and by 1500 hours, Bumpus gave word to start heading back to camp. As if acting on instinct, Jack suddenly yanked Corporal Jim Howard by the collar and threw him fiercely to the ground. With the flick of his rifle point, Jack flipped a thin wire across the trail two feet in front of Howard. Like a catapult, a rope sprung up from the ground and whipped across the path, slamming hard against a wall of wooden spikes carefully concealed in the brush. As quick as he had thrown Howard down, Jack picked him up and motioned him to move on. Jim Howard was frozen in his tracks and just kept staring at the wall of spikes that had his name written all over it. Jack Bumpus stayed at Howard's side for the remainder of the patrol duty until they were returned to friendly lines.

"You got to watch these trails, Son," Bumpus had told him, "the VCs always like to sucker you in on those neat little trails." From that moment on, until he returned to the States, Jim Howard stuck to Jack Bumpus in other combat encounters, and virtually stood by his side. As much as he tried to avoid it, Jack got to know Jim Howard in spite of his reluctance to get too close to any of his men. Jim was different, he had told him when he and Jim said goodbye to each other on Jim's last day in Vietnam. Jim had taken orders well and had performed his military duties with intelligence, Jack had informed him as they shook hands near the landing pad as the helicopter approached for one last time, as far as Jim was concerned.

Jim Howard's mind was far away from Rhode Island now, Father Dick noticed, and the daze that came over him as he related the life-saving tale and the ensuing friendship that developed. Father Dick couldn't help but visualize how frightening the whole experience of the Vietnam War must have been.

"What can I do for you, Father," Jim snapped as if coming out of a hypnotic trance, "Jack's calling in his chit. I wonder how come he isn't taking care of this himself."

Father Dick told Jim that the letter from Jack Bumpus only said that he was unable to personally help because of an illness, which prevented him from making the trip to New England. There was no mention of the nature or extent of the illness but that one other person he could think of, Jim Howard, who, coincidentally, was now in the area, could only address the seriousness of Father Dick's request.

"This must be big, Father, what did you do, steal money from the poor box?" Jim sarcastically replied, knowing that his smart remarks were out of character for him. It was as if the association with Jack Bumpus brought out his crude military past laden with this type of talk. "I'm sorry, Father, a bad joke," quickly shouted Howard, realizing the serious look that was still so evident on Father Dick's face.

Father Dick got up from his chair, stared out the parlor window and, with one hand clasping the crucifix around his neck, turned to Jim Howard.

"I need your help, Mr. Howard. I need someone to help me find my two sons."

CHAPTER 3

Françoise Jeannette Dupont was born June 12, 1932 in Paris, France to Louis and Jacqueline Dupont. The fifth child and only girl, Françoise's birth brought temporary joy to a household struggling to make ends meet in a city beset with poor living and working conditions.

In 1932, Paris was beginning to feel the effects of the world economic depression that started to spread across the globe in 1929 and 1930. Unemployment statistics grew daily and lack of work became a serious problem. There were over six million inhabitants in and around Paris, with the population in the city increasing rapidly from the immigration of Russians, Poles, and Jews driven out by the disturbances present in Eastern Europe. This influx to Paris put additional strain on an already bleak job market.

Louis Dupont was employed as a desk clerk on the night shift at the Hotel Colbert on Rue D'hôtel Colbert. He had been associated with the hotel since he was eighteen years old and held various jobs, first as a janitor and then a bellboy, until becoming a desk clerk at the age of twenty-five. Now, in his early forties, Louis was good at his job, so good that the hotel manager very seldom needed anyone else to assist Louis on his shift. Besides that, Louis had never missed a day of work due to illness and was considered one of the most dependable workers in the hotel. The Hotel Colbert was an old Parisian establishment near the cathedral of Notre Dame and had been in operation for nearly one hundred years. Tradition abounded and the old-fashioned way of catering to the hotel's clientele kept it in competition with many newer hotels cropping up in the city. Louis would never disgrace the hotel in any way and was liked and respected by almost all the other employees as a loyal person and friend.

After his shift ended, usually around 8:00 a.m., Louis would stop at the Bon Marche, a food shop, to check out the daily morning bargains from yesterday's leftovers. It was a long walk for Louis, nearly an hour by the time he had finished at the local shop, to the apartment he rented on the third floor in the Issy section of Paris. He was always warmly greeted by his wife Jacqueline who had herself been up since 5:00 a.m. to feed her pride and joy and only girl, Françoise. She almost looked content in spite of the grueling task of caring for four other growing children, all boys, ranging from sixteen to four, and all four years apart. At thirty-six years old, Jacqueline looked more like fifty. She would await Louis's arrival each morning to sit with him and chat about the upcoming day's activities while he ate his breakfast. The sixteen-year-old was already up and gone to work. A carpenter's helper, Marcel Dupont had been lucky enough to find work on the Exposition grounds near home. The Exposition was to be the site of the 1937 World's Fair and, although five years away, work there was available if you had the skills. Young Marcel had worked for local carpenters for nearly four years and the Exposition job came when local carpentry work was at a virtual standstill because of the poor economy.

Jacqueline would do laundry for the Broussais Hospital, a short distance from home, from 9:00 a.m. until 2:00 p.m. and return home in time to greet the other three boys on their return from school. Louis would watch over Françoise during that time while catching as much sleep as he could. At 2:00 p.m. Louis would be awakened by the gentle touch of his returning wife, who found these few moments each day to be alone with Louis. This was the time when they made love, in the afternoon, the only time they were truly alone to talk of the better days to come when they would have saved enough money to move to a better place, or even to buy their own home outside the city. Fortunately for them, the French government had frozen rents because of the poor times. Every extra franc they earned would be set aside for their dream of better days. But for now, Louis and Jacqueline were content on making ends meet and on using some of the extra money to cater to the newest member of the Dupont family.

At 4:00 p.m. each day, Louis would get ready to leave for his waiter's job at the Café Royal, a job he liked because of the tips he received. Between 5:00 p.m. and 10:00 p.m., Louis could make as much in tips as what he made for a whole night in wages at the hotel. If the café had more business during the day, he would have left the desk clerk's job long ago. As it was, dining in Paris between 5:00 p.m. and 10:00 p.m. was very common and the Café Royal's location between the Hotel-de-Ville and the Hotel-de-Cluny was ideal.

Every Saturday and Sunday, Louis would spend with Françoise, displaying his daughter, like he was wearing a new suit, to his friends and neighbors, as he proudly paraded with her in his arms. The other boys were too busy playing with boys of their own ages in the neighborhood to notice the attention their father gave to Françoise, not that it would have mattered to Louis. This was his pride and joy, his first daughter, and perhaps, his only daughter.

As Françoise grew, Louis would take her to different sections of Paris each weekend, carefully explaining the history of each landmark he pointed out to her. By the time Françoise was six years old, she could identify sites in Paris that her mother did not even know existed. It was quite clear to Louis that this child had a flair for the geography and history of the city and was the first to rise on Saturday so she was ready for the trips throughout the city with her father.

By 1939, the Germans' stronghold on Europe became so obvious that the Parisian government became unsettled. Hitler had invaded and conquered Denmark and Norway and was moving toward France. People in Paris panicked, and the Parisians began to evacuate the city as quickly as they could in a rush to move south to avoid the Germans. The occupation of Paris by the Germans happened so fast that Parisians were left stunned. By June 1940, Paris was an occupied city. The Germans requisitioned the big luxury hotels, splattered swastika flags across famous sights such as the Eiffel Tower, the Arc de Triumphe and major government buildings.

Louis Dupont was still at the Hotel Colbert when the occupation began, but not for long. General Gunther Hausmann, on direct orders from Germany, had taken over the hotel exclusively for the use of German officers and their guests.

"You will not be needed any longer, Dupont," Hausmann said abruptly and without the least bit of concern for this man with a family of seven to feed.

"Louis, what's wrong, what are you doing here?" Jacqueline asked when Louis came home that evening at a few minutes after midnight. Jacqueline had been busy mending and ironing clothes when Louis quietly entered the kitchen.

"The Germans have taken over the hotel and they don't need me anymore. Security reasons. They said that one of their own soldiers would be handling the desk duties from now on. I knew this would happen. We should have left the city when we had a chance to. Now, I don't know what to do," Louis nervously said as he hugged Jacqueline, not wanting her to see the tears building in his eyes.

He composed himself quickly and, as if gaining new strength from within, simply said, "I'll go see Monsieur Cardin at the café tomorrow morning, maybe he can give me more hours at the restaurant."

Unaccustomed to being home in the evening during the week, Louis lay awake most of the night rehearsing his approach with Cardin and his options if there were no more hours for him to work at the café.

The Café Royal was not extending anyone's hours, Cardin had told Louis; in fact, business had dropped so much that he was considering going with less waiters and serving on tables himself. With many Parisians having left the city and few travelers visiting the city, the restaurant business wasn't flourishing. Cardin, a compassionate man with a wife and child himself, knew of Louis' large family and offered to keep Louis on his regular shift. He even was willing to give Louis first coverage when another waiter either left or could not work because of illness. Surely, that would give him some additional hours from time to time. This would mean that Louis had to be available to work at a moment's notice, including Saturdays and Sundays. For Louis, all he could think of was the need to keep his family alive and nourished with a roof over their heads.

The next four years for Françoise were very sad years. She missed her weekend journeys throughout Paris with her father and, because of the resistance movement, stayed close to home at the insistence of her parents. With no sightseeing and no new buildings with a story to be told by her father, Françoise ached at the dull thought of doing housework or helping with her mother's laundry.

In June 1944, Françoise turned twelve years old. Paris had recently avoided being bombed. A Swedish neutral had convinced General von Choltitz of the German army that bombing Paris would serve no purpose. The Allied army was fast approaching and the Germans would soon be forced to surrender the city to the French.

In August of that year, skirmishes broke out between resistance fighters and German troops throughout the city. Choltitz, under orders by Hitler, was to detonate explosives carefully placed under all the monuments of Paris. Realizing the centuries of culture present in these monuments, Choltitz sent a message to the Allied army urging them to move quickly on Paris before other German officers took action he could not be responsible for. General Charles DeGaulle proceeded toward Paris along with General Jacques-Philippe LeClerc, commander of the Second French Armored Division. French troops, not Americans, were to enter the capital first.

On August 25, as the French troops began entering Paris, more fighting broke out with the Germans resulting in serious damage to the Hotel Continental, a short distance away from the Hotel-de-Ville on Rue de Rivoli. Shortly thereafter, the Germans instructed a cease-fire. A surrender had been signed and General DeGaulle was presented to the French people in a victory celebration that evening at the Hotel-de-Ville.

There were tears streaming down Louis Dupont's face as he stood in the crowd below the window of the hotel as the general appeared. Louis beamed. He had once worked at this place. Few people knew the room General DeGaulle appeared in more than Louis. He could describe the furniture, the paintings on the wall, even the design of the curtains in that particular suite. He envisioned himself standing at DeGaulle's side at the window, sharing in the glory that surely was in bloom in the streets below.

The Café Royal was booming with customers now with the return of French and Allied troops to the city and Monsieur Cardin begged Louis to stay at the restaurant. Cardin tried to convince Louis that he would be better off with more hours at the restaurant than at the hotel because it would allow him to be home with his family each night and on weekends as well. Louis was loyal; he had been loyal for all the years he had been at the hotel, and he had no intention of leaving Cardin when he needed him. After all, wasn't this the man who kept Louis' family with food during the war years by offering him work, even when business was poor? How could he turn his back on him now? Indeed, Louis would stay at the Café Royal and, in appreciation, Cardin made Louis his maître d' and headwaiter.

Françoise, most of all, was elated at the news that her father was now going to be home on weekends, those glorious weekends of exploring the attractions of Paris with her giant of a father. "This Saturday, Papa, can we just walk through the city again," pleaded Françoise, "it's been so long since I've seen any buildings outside this street that I don't know if I'll remember them."

Louis smiled and warmly responded, "Little one, as soon as your eyes come upon a sight you have seen but once before, you will remember not only its name but the whole history behind it as I once told you."

Paris was alive again and the streets were bustling with soldiers and traffic, as Françoise had never seen before. As they walked on the Rue de Vanves toward Avenue du Maine, Françoise began, "There's the Institut Pasteur de Montrouge and over there is the Cimetiere du Montparnasse and..." she continued like the rapid fire of a machine gun, spitting out information in succession as if she had seen these landmarks the day before, not four years ago.

If he had any doubts about her remembering the lessons he had taught her about the city and its sights, Françoise convinced her father in the first hour that, not only did she remember, she craved for more. It was just Françoise and her father, no brothers to tease her, no mother to subject her to the routine of housework, and the freedom to roam on and on in a city that seemed to offer more each time she thought she had seen it all.

By noon they had meandered through the streets, stopping briefly to talk about the buildings and even going inside a few to see if the bombings had badly damaged any of them. They approached the Café Royal where Louis had planned for them to stop for a quick lunch as the restaurant prepared to open for the day. Monsieur Cardin and the other employees who knew that Louis held a special place of importance at the restaurant greeted him with warmth. Waiters and chefs were immediately attracted to Françoise's smile and eagerness to learn about everything around her and spoiled Françoise at lunch.

As time went on, the Saturday lunches at the café were times when each waiter could sit briefly with Françoise to tell her about other parts of Paris she had not seen, or so they thought. Each week became a testing period for her as she anxiously awaited the quizzing from the waiters on the sites of Paris. And every time, the waiters would come away shaking their heads in amazement at Françoise's phenomenal memory for detail, even when the questions concerned small out-of-the-way monuments she had not even visited yet.

The next four years were very prosperous ones for the Dupont family. Louis had been promoted to restaurant manager as Monsieur Cardin worked less and less due to arthritis in his legs forcing him to stay off them more and more. Cardin would sit behind the counter and act as the cashier while Louis would oversee the entire operation of the restaurant.

At ages fifty-seven and fifty-three, Louis and his wife had finally realized the dream of owning their own home.

A small cottage just outside of the city was all they needed now that all the other children were grown and on their own, except Françoise, at seventeen, who was completing her schooling and still living at home. Louis had purchased a car, but the drive to the restaurant was too much bother each day. In 1949, parking on public thoroughfares was tolerated by the police even though it was in violation of public laws prohibiting it. The congestion on the city streets made Louis nervous since he had only recently begun to drive an automobile. It was, for Louis, a status symbol more than a means of transport. Instead, he would take the Metro from just outside the city limits and would leave the car at home if Jacqueline needed it.

Jacqueline was no longer working, there was no need to, and she proudly spent her days in her new garden where she planted flowers and nurtured them as she had done with her children. Although only fifty-three years old, she looked well into her sixties. The early years of struggle to keep her family alive had taken their toll on her. Her eyesight was failing, her figure became noticeably plump and she had an increasingly difficult time in keeping her weight down due to her more relaxed lifestyle.

Weekends for Louis were now without Françoise who knew her way around Paris far better than her father. He had taught her well and she had not been content with only what her father had shown her. It wasn't enough; Françoise was like an engine that required more and more fuel to keep it running. In her case, the fuel was a new site, an old building, and another piece of history about the city.

Françoise had applied to be a tour guide with Le Bourget, the Paris airport for international travelers.

Throughout recent years, she had learned to speak English quite well and was studying to become an interpreter for the French government. Le Bourget was getting so much traffic from people abroad that it needed more guides to explain the sights of Paris on its bus tours that picked up tourists at various hotels in the city.

At first, the tour director was hesitant at hiring a seventeen-year-old girl for a position requiring an older, more seasoned person. After some preliminary testing by the director, he simply asked, "Do you know where the Place de L'Etoile is located?" Françoise smiled and said, "La Place de L'Etoile was constructed in 1854 in Neuilly and originally was the focal point where five avenues intersected. Hausmann, the engineer, made it a circle in later years where twelve avenues now meet. In 1860, Hottorf, the architect, constructed twelve identical town houses bordering the circle. You would reach the monument by way of Boulevard Hausmann, named after its engineer.." Françoise conducted her first tour that Saturday.

For the next two years, Françoise would conduct tours on weekends and every day during the summer months. She had completed her formal schooling and was now earning a good salary as Paris underwent major renovations and tourism continued to flourish. Traffic congestion forced improvements to the Metro and train system. Poor water and sewer systems forced the government to speed the development of better housing facilities with improved water treatment facilities. Ever changing, Paris was her life, Françoise reflected, as she proudly pointed out the new and how it blended in nicely with the old during her tours.

Françoise had matured into a very attractive woman of nineteen by the spring of 1951. Her long brown hair radiated from her face and brought out the beauty of her facial features. Blue eyes, a smooth and radiant complexion without a blemish, teeth that emanated a warm smile each time she spoke, and a statuesque body with perfect curves in all the right places. She had grown to feel not only the yearning of the city but also the desires of the heart. More so in recent months than before, it was as if a flower had suddenly blossomed and young males could now see the body beneath the smile. She had reached the time in her life when she began to think of love and romance and what it would be like to be with a man.

The tour bus was loaded on this August morning. The driver of the bus, Rejean Boiteau, was a quiet man in his early twenties who had recently joined the company. He had just moved to Paris from Dijon where life for a young man was not as exciting or as promising as in Paris. Françoise entered the bus and immediately introduced herself to the passengers, ignoring Rejean as she faced her eager students of the city.

"We will today cover the main attractions of Paris, stopping at each one to allow time for photographs and to walk inside some of the buildings. Please do not go off on your own since we will not stay long at any one location except for lunch at the Café Royal. If there are any questions I can answer, please ask. I will try to tell you as much about Paris as I can," she said as she motioned to the driver to begin the tour by heading down Rue du Temple. It was then that she noticed the new driver. "You're not the normal driver, where's Maurice?"

"I am Rejean and I am taking Maurice's place today. He is not feeling well and the director said you were the best person to start driving with on these tours. I will need some help though, I don't know my way around the streets yet," said Rejean.

Françoise smiled, as she always did, and introduced herself as she pointed out the direction he should proceed. As the bus slowly made its way through the maze of Paris, Françoise could feel Rejean's eyes gazing at her at each stop. He was a terrible driver and had difficulty shifting the grinding gears of the bus, jerking it forward after every stop, and bouncing over the curbing at nearly every corner he made. This made it difficult for her to concentrate on her presentation to the tourists and Françoise began to get visibly irritated with these distractions.

"Please be more careful at what you're doing," she pointed out to him, "this is intended to be a way to enjoy the sights of the city, not a bumpy ride all over the streets."

Rejean could not help himself. He was distracted by her every move and the slender lines of her body as she stood there next to him. The faint aroma from her cologne added to the urges he began to feel building inside of him. By the time the tour had reached the Café Royal, Françoise was so visibly upset with the terrible ride her passengers had just gone through that she apologized to them, explaining that the remainder of the tour after lunch would most definitely improve.

As the tourists exited the bus and entered the café, Françoise greeted her father and immediately proceeded to the public telephone at the rear of the restaurant.

"Hello, Françoise, what can I do for you, you didn't get into an accident did you?" asked the director of the tour company.

"No, no, Monsieur Pontbriand, I am afraid we will be getting many complaints from the people on this tour," Françoise explained. "The new driver you gave me is driving badly and the passengers are not able to enjoy the ride. I don't think it is good for business if they tell other people at their hotels to stay away from our tours."

"Where are you now, Françoise," grumbled Pontbriand. "I will send another man over. The new boy is not experienced enough to drive in the city. I'll send him instead on the tour that goes outside the city tomorrow. Let me talk to him."

Françoise spotted Rejean already sitting at a table in the corner by himself. Françoise wondered if he sat alone because he was shy or because the passengers were furious with him from the morning's bad ride. She motioned for him to come to the telephone because Monsieur Pontbriand wanted to speak to him and moved on to one of the tables where the tour passengers were seated.

Louis would always watch his daughter as she mingled with the patrons and he was pleased at how confident she had grown in her work. Monsieur Cardin had on several occasions thanked Françoise for arranging the tours so that they would stop at his restaurant for lunch each day. The small commission he had agreed to give the tour company for the extra business still brought many tourists to the café, tourists who often returned on other days, and mostly in the company of other friends. Monsieur Cardin had grown as fond of Françoise as everyone else.

"You pig, you lousy little bitch," screamed Rejean as he darted straight toward Françoise. "You couldn't give me a chance, could you? You had to call Monsieur Pontbriand on my very first day. I hope you're happy now; I'll probably lose my job and I can't afford to."

"Monsieur Pontbriand assured me you would be used on another bus until you know the city better. It's for your own good. You were making the passengers nervous and without them you won't have a job anyway." Françoise said as she tried to calm him down before he made a scene and added to his already shaky start with the tourists.

In a fit of contempt, Rejean shoved Françoise aside and stormed out the door. She fell to the floor and her face turned red.

At a nearby table, a young man swiftly jumped to his feet and extended his hand to Françoise to help her up. As she still had her eyes on the door as the young driver bolted out, the helping hand motioned for Françoise to sit down at that table, occupied also by an elderly couple.

"Are you hurt, mademoiselle?" the concerned young man asked.

Françoise motioned to everyone that she was fine and attempted to compose herself with a few sips of wine from a glass placed before her by the young man. "Merci, merci beaucoup, monsieur, I am sorry for this trouble, I have never had this happen before," she explained. "It is not good for you to have this happen to you, you are only here to enjoy the city, not to be insulted by this behavior."

No problem, really," smiled the young man as he sipped his own glass of wine. "To tell you the truth, it's the most excitement I've had since I arrived in Europe last week. I'm only sorry you had to be the victim."

Louis had already reached the table and was shaken at the thought of someone striking his Françoise. Once he was reassured that she was not hurt, he motioned to a waiter to be certain that her table was well taken care of throughout lunch.

"Well, shall we order, mademoiselle," said the young man as he smiled again at Françoise. "What do you suggest? Oh, by the way, this is Mr. and Mrs. Quinlan from New York, and I'm Richard from Vermont. Richard Merrill."

CHAPTER 4

Richard Arthur Merrill was born in April 1926 in Rumney, New Hampshire, the son of Charles and Alice Merrill. The Merrills were lifelong residents of New Hampshire and lived in a farmhouse on a plateau at the foot of some mountainous terrain near Tenney Mountain. Charlie Merrill's hens produced enough eggs to sell as far away as Plymouth, nearly a ten-mile ride in his old beat-up Ford pickup truck.

Every day he would make his rounds in Plymouth, stopping at the two restaurants, the local hospital, and the college on the hill to deliver almost all the eggs he had. What few he didn't sell, he would bring back home to Alice so she could make pies and cakes to sell at the same establishments on the next day's trip. When Charlie delivered his eggs, he would ask his customers what kind of cakes or pies they would need and when. Alice could bake practically anything they asked for and, depending on the season, the requests for her baked goods were almost always met on time, even if Alice had to spend late hours finishing someone's orders for the next day. It was no wonder that the Merrill house always had a wonderful aroma to it, unlike the typical dairy farms where the smell of manure permeated the premises.

Farms in that central part of the state were some distance apart and Dick Merrill's childhood was filled with a lot of solitude. The few friends he made were from school where a dozen or so children from the village were to be educated. Classes were mixed together and there was only one teacher, Miss Merriweather. She was a local woman in her fifties who had never married and lived alone in the house she had been born in, a few minutes away from the schoolhouse.

In the winter, when snowstorms came, as they often did, Dick Merrill would not go to school because the roads to the schoolhouse became impassable. On those days, he would help his father clear a path from the farm to the main road leading to Plymouth so that the delivery truck could be used for deliveries. Another good year, Charlie Merrill thought, would be all he needed to afford buying a plow for his truck so that he and Dick wouldn't be wasting time shoveling when they could be selling. And besides, Charlie had it all figured out, he could use the truck to plow out businesses when deliveries were done and earn enough to expand the business.

The Merrills had no other children even though they had tried for years. Dick's parents were both forty-five years old when he was born and the Merrills had all but given up on having children when word had come from Doc Hinkson that Alice was pregnant.

The Merrills' farm was big in acreage but small in what was on the land itself. There were three hen houses holding about five hundred laying hens that each produced one to two eggs per day. The farmhouse was about two hundred feet in front of the coops and had only five rooms, the kitchen being the biggest. Alice had three stoves that she used constantly to bake her goods and a small kitchen table and counter area for the family to use when they sat at mealtime. The kitchen led to an open double parlor with one side being used by Charlie for his office and records and the far end with a wood stove, rug on the floor, and a parlor set complete with an old Emerson stand-up radio. Upstairs, there were two bedrooms and a new bathroom with running water from a pump that Charlie had recently installed.

Sundays were always special for the Merrills. After the early chores in the hen houses and a special breakfast prepared by Alice for her two boys, the family would dress up in their best clothing and head to church. There were not too many Catholic churches in New Hampshire and the Merrills had to drive clear to the southern side of Plymouth to reach St. Barnaby's for eleven o'clock Mass. Charlie's father had come over from Ireland at the turn of the century and had been determined to continue his family in the Catholic faith.

Alice, a local girl before marrying Charlie, converted to Catholicism only because the church insisted on it to allow the marriage to take place. She did not care that much what religion it was, so long as there was some spiritual bond that could keep the family together when they needed it. Charlie, like his father before him, was going to raise Dick to follow the faith of his ancestors; it just had to be that way. It was no surprise then when Charlie asked Alice to stop by the general store one Sunday to pick up some cloth. The cloth was to make altar boy cassocks for Dick since he had been selected by Father Gavin to become a junior altar boy at St. Barnaby's.

As the years went by, Dick became more and more involved with the church. He had seen Father Gavin working on the church grounds often as he drove past the church on special deliveries that went that way. He had grown fond of Father Gavin and saw him as just a regular person who had chosen the priesthood as his occupation. He did everything else other people did, except maybe get married and raise a family.

Business was prospering and Charlie had added a second delivery truck with a full-time driver. Although the demand for eggs was thriving and that segment of the business was going as well as ever, it was the pie and cake business that was growing at an unbelievable rate. By the time Dick had reached the age of fifteen, in the early 1940s, Charlie Merrill's business had grown to the point where Alice could not bake enough pies or cakes fast enough to keep up with the demand. Every resort restaurant in the White Mountain area of New Hampshire carried her pastries, which now carried the name Merrill's Fresh Baked on each individually labeled package. Local stores carried the Merrill brand too and, as home-baking trends began to disappear with more women working in the Plymouth parachute factory, housewives now referred to Merrill's pies and cakes as "almost like my own."

Dick had done well in school and Miss Merriweather had already spoken to Dick's parents about sending him to college following graduation.

Charlie had mixed feelings about the news. He had always expected Dick to join him in the family business on a full-time basis. The business was successful enough to support Charlie and Dick, with Charlie thinking about slowing down a bit as he approached his retirement years. Alice, on the other hand, wanted her son to have a better life without having to work the strenuous hours that were required in the business. She had visualized Dick as a doctor, a lawyer, even a priest, someone who would help people in trouble. Dick's gentle and friendly manner was something that automatically emanated as he dealt with customers, school friends, or other active parishioners from St. Barnaby's.

"You'll be finishing your schooling soon, Son," Charlie began one evening at supper, "Have you given any thought to what you'd like to do with your life?" Charlie leaned forward, his eyebrows raised as he awaited Dick's reply. He was hopeful of a decision to join him in running the farm. Alice knew anything else was going to be a disappointment. Dick's mother was more reserved and subdued as she quietly passed the roast to Charlie and reached for the mashed potatoes.

"Can we afford college, Dad?" Dick questioned. "I was thinking of going to Plymouth Teachers in the fall if I get accepted there. Father Gavin and Miss Merriweather both told me that I should consider it, if we can afford it. Father Gavin said that when he went to college, he didn't know what he wanted either but it gave him time to think while he was getting more education. That sounds logical to me," Dick said. "Father Gavin said that the experience from school could be put to good use whatever I decide to do. What do you think?" Dick asked.

"I think Father Gavin's been filling your head with big ideas on colleges, and that's not what I had expected from him. I figured he'd want to steer you to be a priest or something like that," Charlie quickly snapped back at his son. "Why does he care so much about what happens to you?"

"I like Father Gavin, Dad; he's helped me to eliminate the things I don't want to do in my life, and now I'm just trying to narrow it down some more. I'm not going in the Army, Dad," Dick quickly shot back. "There's no way I'm going to get involved with killing people. I love my country, but I won't kill anyone. God didn't bring me into this world to kill people. I want to do some good for people and I think college education will give me time to decide what I want to do. And besides, I want to meet more people my own age, maybe even go with girls, I don't know."

Charlie just sat there, expressionless and kept on eating his food as if Dick had said nothing. It usually worked, the silent treatment, at least it always had before. Charlie figured that when you don't say anything, it's as good as or better than arguing with someone. He merely would express his opinion and, if Dick disagreed or argued against Charlie's views, Charlie would use the silent treatment.

"The silent treatment won't work this time, Dad, if we can't afford it, then I'll get myself another job this summer and start saving until I have enough to go. I've got to find out if it's for me."

"You ain't gonna make no more money just because you went to college, you know. Why don't you wait awhile before going off to school; give me a couple of years in the business. If it doesn't work out then, I'll agree to send you to school wherever you want to go."

Dick's mother sat through the meal, never once uttering a sound. She had made several trips to the stove and the kitchen sink with dishes and had heard the entire conversation. Charlie was the man of the house, she had been told by her mother years before, and she never interfered with him when the conversation was with Dick. She would wait until Charlie went to bed a short while later and would then wait for Dick to return to the kitchen. He always did when he and Charlie disagreed on something. He would try to explain his side to his mother in the hope of gaining her support for a comeback to Charlie the following day. Sometimes Alice would soften the way with Charlie by persuading him to reconsider. Most of the time it worked but, on certain occasions, Alice could be as firm as Charlie. She had a mind of her own.

On this night, she saw the tremendous disappointment in Dick's face as he rose from the supper table and quietly walked to the hallway, grabbed his jacket and motioned over his shoulder, "I'm going for a walk, be back in a little while."

It was cold that November night in 1943 as Dick Merrill walked along the dark road from the farmhouse to the main road. He never expressed his anger or frustration in front of others. He kept his feelings to himself and preferred to be alone to collect his thoughts. His parents were trying to keep him home, not because they didn't want him to go to college, they just didn't want to let go. Dick was nearly a man, nearly eighteen years old, and he had never dated a girl or been outside of New Hampshire. As a matter of fact, he didn't even know many girls except Sally Anderson. Sally lived in Plymouth and went to high school there. She was seventeen, a year younger than Dick, but she too was graduating in June, just seven months away. Dick would frequently sit and talk with Sally over a soda at the Hillside Diner in Plymouth where Dick had made several deliveries. She was going to Plymouth Teachers College in the fall and often tried to encourage Dick to do the same. It would be great, he had thought, Sally is not like other girls, she doesn't try to flirt with people as girls tended to do. Dick liked Sally as a nice person to be with just to talk to and share ideas with. She had a boyfriend who was already away at school at the university in Durham. He had graduated from high school the year before and would write to Sally each week. She would tell Dick about some of the exciting things that went on at college from the letters her boyfriend wrote.

Alice was getting worried. Dick had never stayed out this late on one of his walks. Charlie had gone to bed, the supper dishes had been washed and dried, and the pastries for the next day's deliveries were all boxed and ready to go. It was ten o'clock, very late for a school night, she thought. Alice knew the difficulty Dick was having in deciding what he was going to do come graduation time. She also knew that the farm and the business were not for him. Sure, he would always work hard at his chores and in making deliveries. But she could see that he only did it to help his father. He would rather be at school or at St. Barnaby's or alone listening to the birds sing or walking up the mountain on weekends.

Noise from the squeaky hallway door springs brought a smile and a sigh of relief to Alice's worried face. She knew that Dick would be walking in once he removed his jacket. Dick didn't head for the kitchen as Alice had expected and as he had always done before when he needed to get advice on a problem or a disagreement with his father. Instead, he headed up the stairs straight for his room. Alice was deeply concerned. She knew that Dick was no longer satisfied with just obeying his father and accepting his wishes. It wasn't that Dick didn't love his father and it wasn't that Charlie merely took advantage of his son's work for all of these years. Alice knew that Charlie would give his right arm for his son if it were necessary. She also knew that Charlie had never faced the possibility of Dick leaving the farm one day, and he was as confused about Dick's future as Dick was himself. One thing Alice knew for certain, Dick had to make this decision and only Dick. Charlie's dream of having his son in the business had to be Dick's dream also, and it wasn't.

Alice folded the newspaper she had been glancing at on and off for almost two hours and switched off the small light in the kitchen as she headed up the stairs to bed. As she passed Dick's room in the darkened corridor, she could hear him talking in his room. His bedroom door was slightly open and Alice stopped to listen to what he was saying. Dick's bed was behind the doorway as you went in and Alice did not dare go in as all she could see was a ray of light shining on the floor from the moonlit window.

"Dear Lord," the voice was saying, "help me to find the way. My love for them is the only thing I have, except for you. I can't desert them now and, yet, I want so much to learn more about the world that I have to go. How do I tell them?" His voice was mellowing now and he was nearly asleep, "Somehow I know you will show me the way."

Charlie rolled over when Alice got in bed beside him. He was restless. Alice knew he'd be half awake when she entered the room. Whenever Charlie and Dick had serious arguments or when Charlie had to go to the bank the following day for a loan, he usually could not sleep. He could see the glimmer of Alice's face as she lay by his side staring at the ceiling as if to be a thousand miles away. Her cheeks were filled with tears as she just lay there, motionless. They did not speak, they did not face each other, but they both knew. Dick would be gone by the end of the summer.

* * *

As the months passed and spring arrived, Dick's silence and more frequent periods of solitude became unbearable for Alice.

"We have to talk," Alice quietly began as she served dinner. "Dick's going to graduate from school in June and that's only three months away," Alice continued, looking straight at Charlie. "He wants to go to college and he's got the good grades to show for it. Are you two gonna talk to each other about this, or are you gonna keep on chewing up inside until the both of you can't stand it anymore?"

"Alice, this ain't your affair. This here is between Dick and me and it doesn't concern you. Besides, I didn't think there was anything to discuss. We agreed he would stay here and learn the business for a couple of years before deciding to do anything," Charlie said as his eyes shifted from Alice to Dick.

"Well, to tell you the truth, Dad," Dick meekly responded, "there sort of is something I'd like to."

Before he had a chance to finish his sentence, Alice snapped back, "Like hell it's none of my business, Charlie Merrill; it's as much my business and he's as much my son as he is yours. The fact is, you stubborn ass, your son wants to go to college bad, or at least to try it, and you can't see the forest for the trees. He doesn't want this life for himself, Charlie. Is that so bad? Just because it's been good to us don't mean it's gonna be good for him. When are you gonna let him make up his own mind? He's gonna be eighteen, for God's sake!"

There was fire in Alice's eyes, a rage that Dick had never seen before. This couldn't be his sweet, quiet mother who never raised her voice at anyone, except maybe once when one of the drivers had dropped and ruined two dozen of her pies while loading the truck.

This was different. This outburst was with Charlie. Never had his parents argued in front of him. The Merrills didn't think it was good for children to see parents yelling at each other. If they had done so before, Dick had never heard it. But he was hearing it now and he just sat there with his mouth open and could just say, "Mom, Mom, calm down, I was going to bring it up myself."

"No, you weren't; you would rather be miserable and do anything that your father wants, even though he doesn't realize how much you're hurting, Son," Alice pleaded as tears started pouring from her eyes. "You can't keep it in forever, Dick; I won't stand another minute of this. No mother could ask for a better son all these years. It isn't right for you to miss out on things anymore. I know there's not much out here to make life exciting, but your father and me, that's the way we want it. It don't mean you gotta put up with living out here. There's so much of this country out there, Son. Find what you're looking for. God knows you won't find it here."

"I've been quiet long enough on this, Charlie, maybe too long. We don't need any more trucks right now, and even if we did, what's more important, your son's future or a stupid truck?" she continued, tears running down her cheeks as if she were standing in the rain. "I won't let you do this, Charlie; I won't let you decide for him what he has to decide for himself. We can afford it and you know it. We're not poor; we have more than most folks around here. Look at him, Charlie, look at him, can't you see it in his face, can't you hear him begging you with his silence?"

Charlie's eyes met Dick's and for once he knew that Alice was right. He loved his son more dearly than anything. Don't you protect the ones you love, he thought? Was he so wrong in wanting to keep his son by his side, even for just a little while longer? Why couldn't things stay the same? Why did Dick have to grow up? It isn't fair, he thought, the world's taking him away from me and I can't stop it.

"Son," Charlie said as he reached across the table and placed his hand on Dick's. "I should have known your heart wasn't in this place, I should have seen it, Son, but I didn't want to. You're all we have and we won't lose you over this. If you really got your mind set on trying more schooling, then it's done. There's no way you couldn't make us proud of you. I'm sorry it took so long for me to see it," Charlie said as he gently stroked Alice's cheek, wiping her tears away with his other hand. She smiled and grabbed his hand and kissed it and reached out to Dick's arm as the three of them just sat there for what seemed like hours.

* * *

Graduation came fast and the months seemed to fly by that summer of 1944. For his eighteenth birthday, Dick had been given a complete set of new clothes and an old pickup truck to use to travel the distance to and from Plymouth Teachers College.

Plymouth Teachers College was an old school founded in 1839 and focused on educating future teachers. It was located in the center of town, with about four thousand residents year-round and a vacation spot for thousands more. Plymouth's beautiful valley setting had made it an ideal place for summer vacations and for travelers visiting the White Mountains. As the area grew in popularity and traffic, there sprouted more and more restaurants, lodges, and inns to accommodate them. All of these hospitality facilities offered meals and the local products sold under the Merrill name were a natural.

Dick's first year at Plymouth was a difficult one. Although he commuted to Plymouth each day from home, he had never been involved in an atmosphere with so many people before and, to suddenly be in the midst of it all, was awkward. He became conscious of his appearance, new wardrobe or not, and had to work very hard at opening up in his new surroundings. Dick had decided to major in History and was planning on teaching young children when he graduated. While volunteering for work at St. Barnaby's over the last few years, Dick had grown fond of assisting Father Gavin in his religion classes to the youngsters every Saturday morning during the school year. He found the Bible stories that the children were read to be a peaceful but effective way to teach them about

God and the other saints. It was from these sessions that Dick felt most at ease in talking to people and, as he participated more and more in the religion classes, he gained confidence in speaking before other groups as well.

On Sundays, Dick now served as a lector at Mass at St. Barnaby's and, to tourists, it was hard to tell that Dick was not a priest when he wore his cassock. In May of 1945, at the end of his first year of college, Dick had matured into a well-spoken and handsome man. He had mushroomed to well over six feet tall and had the physique of an athlete, although he had never found any great interest in participating in sports. He enjoyed swimming and hiking, and still went off on his long treks up the mountain on weekends, oftentimes taking a few schoolbooks with him. He would find a picturesque spot at the top of the mountain and plop himself against a tree and read for hours. It was solace for Dick since the conversation at home with his father was strained as Charlie still believed that Dick was better off on the farm than at school. Dinners at home were fairly quiet, almost as if Charlie resented the fact that Dick had won this battle.

Dick was returning from his mountain on an afternoon in May when he noticed a great deal of commotion as he appeared from the trail leading back to the farm at the rear of their property. The swirling red lights at the side of the house, at this time of day as the sun began to set, could be seen for miles. His heart started to beat faster as his instincts told him immediately that something was wrong. "Oh, my God, no, please, no, not Mom," he thought out loud as he began to run faster and faster to reach home. "She must be hurt, she burned herself at the stoves, she's been working too hard lately, I knew it," he ranted as he kept on running, faster and faster, until he reached the ambulance that signaled fright and pain.

"It's your father, Dick," Alice spoke as he rushed through the kitchen door. "He was just sitting here with me talking about how things seemed to have worked out so well and talking about retiring soon. Then, all of a sudden, his face grew pale, like he was mad, and he grabbed his chest with both hands like a knife had been put to him," Alice continued, gripping tightly on Dick's arm as if to hang on. "I didn't know what to do; I called Doc Hinkson and he's with him now."

Almost in the same motion as his mother finished speaking, Dick was heading for the sofa in the parlor where Doc Hinkson and two other men were huddled over Charlie. One man was pumping furiously over Charlie while the doctor was rubbing his elbow with rubbing alcohol on a gauze, preparing to inject Charlie with some solution.

Alice held her son back, "You can't do anything for him, Dick, it's up to somebody else now," she moaned, staring into her son's drawn face. They held each other tightly and Dick cried uncontrollably as Alice cradled him in her arms.

Charlie had suffered a massive heart attack and never regained consciousness. He was to be buried three days later under an elm tree in a grove on the farm near the trail leading up the mountain.

Father Gavin was to perform the service at St. Barnaby's and his mother asked Dick if he would say the eulogy for his father. Father Gavin knew that Dick had become a good speaker in front of groups, but this would be different. The church was filled with friends, relatives, and acquaintances of the Merrills and this would be his father he was going to talk about. Dick had not left his mother's side since Charlie had been stricken. Two nights before the funeral, Alice asked Dick to sit with her in the parlor; she had something important to discuss with him.

"Your father had been doing a lot of thinking in the last few months," she began, "and he was getting tired a lot lately. He wanted to slow down and maybe even do a little traveling this summer. Charlie hadn't seen his brother, your uncle Sean, in almost ten years when he came up last summer to see us on his vacation. Your uncle Sean never liked the cold weather and, with his arthritis, always was glad he had moved to Florida. When your father realized that you weren't about to take over the business in a couple of years, he talked about selling it all, the farm too, to a big bakery in Nashua. They made an offer that he was really thinking about, more money than we'd ever seen in our entire lives." Alice walked over to the desk in the adjoining office area and reached for some papers on Charlie's desk. As she approached Dick, Alice said, "Your father signed the agreement three days ago and told me about it the day before he died. He was going to tell you that night at supper. I could see a sense of relief when he told me, like a big load had been taken off him. He even smiled when he told me," Alice continued, "if only I'd known, but Doc Hinkson said there was no way I could've known, Charlie hardly ever complained about anything."

Dick started reading the papers his mother had just given him and looked up at her in a daze. "What are you going to do, Mom, where are you going to go? I'm still here; I'll run the business if you want to stay." uttered Dick as he rose to his feet.

"No, Son, you're gonna go back to school where you belong, except now you're gonna live in Plymouth at the school and, come vacation time, you can come down to Florida to live with me."

"Florida? You're moving to Florida, who are you going to know down there, except Uncle Sean?"

"Your Uncle Sean and Aunt Jean were planning on opening their own little restaurant in Boca Raton, right near the ocean, and your father and I had sort of agreed to go in with them. I called Sean yesterday and he'll be here tomorrow to help me get some of these things straightened out," Alice went on, "and your uncle Sean doesn't need any money. He just wants me to come down there, live with them for a while until I find my own place and then, maybe do some cooking at the restaurant if I want."

"I'm nearly sixty-five years old and I can't take care of this place by myself, nor do I want to. And I don't want you here either. I'm tired of pushing and pushing to make a bigger business. It's time for me to slow down and see some of the world out there. I haven't been out of New Hampshire in over twenty years. "Your father once told me he probably wouldn't get to see the sun set anywhere but here before he died. I didn't know then just how true that statement would turn out to be."

As expected, on the day of Charlie's funeral, St. Barnaby's was packed with mourners who had known Charlie Merrill for nearly fifty years. Whether it was out of mere business courtesy or genuine sorrow for the loss of a dear friend, they all came. Father Gavin had paid particular attention to all the details personally. Somehow the attachment to his young pupil for several years compelled him to reach for that extra ounce of energy to show his compassion for Dick's father in the only way he could.

The pews were lined with a delegation from the Knights of Columbus dressed in their navy blue uniforms complete with feathered hats. There were bouquets of flowers surrounding the entire vestibule. Father Gavin had summoned all of the altar boys from the local school to attend, dressed in full cassocks as they stood in rows near the church choir to the left of the sacristy. The altar was draped with rich white cloth and more flowers. It looked more like a royal wedding than a funeral.

The time soon came for Dick to deliver the eulogy. He had not discussed it nor allowed anyone to read it. It was to be his thoughts about his father and he was going to say them as he wrote them. As he approached the lectern, he glanced at Father Gavin seated behind the altar. Father Gavin was clutching the crucifix hanging around his neck with his left hand while, at the same time, signaled a sign of the cross toward Dick with his right hand.

As Dick placed his prepared talk on the lectern, he noticed a simple message taped to the facing. It read: I am with you, Dick, do not despair.

"Most of you," Dick began, "have known my father much longer than I have, for my mother and he gave birth to me when they were both already forty-five years old. Before I was born, I am told that my father would spend his mornings making his egg deliveries and, the afternoons he would spend at the bar of the Plymouth Bar & Grille talking about his dreams of someday being rich and famous. My mother," Dick continued as he looked down toward Alice's teary-eyed face, "she never complained, so the story goes, when he stumbled in each night, sometimes too drunk to even sit for the meal she had worked hard to prepare for him. This went on for nearly ten years, I am told, ten years. And then on April 25, 1925, it stopped. That's the day I was born. From that day on until today, I have never seen my father take a drink anywhere. I am told that he had a purpose in life now that he had a son. My mother and father had been married for twenty years when I was born, and I was the first and only child. It seems, so the story goes, that my father had made a promise to God that, if Charlie and Alice Merrill could have a child, he would change." He smiled at his mother as he continued.

"I tell you this today because the father I knew is the one I will always remember. The Charlie Merrill you have known is the one who proved to you that faith in God can do pretty wonderful things. I never knew Charlie Merrill, the drinker, and I probably would never have known about my father's depressing past until someone sat me down last June and told me all about it. It was something I had to know. You're better off hearing it from me, my father told me, than from somebody who's only going to give you pieces of the story. So, Charlie Merrill sat me down on my graduation day under an elm tree in a grove at the foot of his mountain and told me what a bum he had been for years until I was born."

"God sent me to them and now He's taken him back," Dick went on with sorrow in his voice, "I thank God for letting me have such wonderful parents. As much as I will miss my father, it is my mother who has suffered more over the years, the good ones and the very bad ones, than anyone else. And now, comes the cruelest blow of them all, just when they were both to begin enjoying their retirement, he has been taken from her. My father once told me, expect nothing and you'll never be disappointed. My mother will survive because she is strong, strong in faith that God's will must be done. I will miss you, Dad, more than you know and more than I could ever tell you when you were alive. I won't see you for a while," his voice began to crack and his emotion was overtaking him now, "but someday we'll all be together again. So long, Dad, until we meet again."

Silence. Not a sound could be heard throughout the church, not a cough, not a whimper, only to be broken by the sound of noses blowing throughout. Dick caressed the casket as he descended from the lectern to return to his mother's side. Alice cradled her arms around Dick's and gently leaned her head to rest on his shoulder.

At that moment she knew. Mothers have a way of knowing. Call it a sixth sense, ESP, or clairvoyance, whatever, but when it comes to mothers and their children, there is something there that telegraphs messages on things that others can't pick up. Alice knew her son. She had seen the torment on his face on more than one occasion and she saw it again this day. This was to be no ordinary man who sat beside her. How could she have not seen it before? There was her son, majestic as could be, standing over his audience and speaking with such eloquence that people were moved to tears. It was then that Alice realized that Dick would someday become a priest, a man of God; it was just a matter of time. Dick would not return to Plymouth Teachers College.

CHAPTER 5

The agreement between the Merrills and Nashua Foods was finalized several weeks later. Sean Merrill had called in an attorney from Boston to consummate the transaction and to set up various bank accounts and investments as Alice had requested. Alice's accounts would be held at the First Bank & Trust in Boston. She would have a checking account set up to draw against her funds at will and would receive a monthly accounting statement at Sean's address in Florida.

The farm and the business had been sold for $150,000. Alice had placed $50,000 in the bank account and had set up a special trust fund for the remaining $100,000, with the provision that the account be in her name until her death or Dick's twenty-fifth birthday, whichever came first. Alice knew that with modest, conservative interest added to the account each year, Dick would never need worry about money again. She did not tell Dick about the trust account, choosing instead to merely relate to him that she was financially stable enough to afford living very comfortable for the rest of her life and still have enough to allow Dick to complete his college years.

* * *

The day finally came that July morning when Dick and his mother were set to leave the Merrill farm for the last time. Dick had already made arrangements to keep his pick-up truck at St. Barnaby's over the remaining summer months until he returned for his second year at Plymouth Teachers College. By noon, most of the furniture and personal belongings had been packed and loaded in the moving van. Except for the kitchen stoves and refrigerator and some of Charlie's office furniture, which was included in the sale of the farm, the house resembled any other home in transition. Nashua Foods had decided to convert the farm into a regional office, serving not only the Merrill brand of pastries and eggs, but using the remainder of the property to erect a distribution center for the company's other line of products.

Alice had insisted that the contract with Nashua include a clause requiring Nashua to preserve and isolate the grave site area where Charlie was buried and to allow the site to also be her own grave site alongside her husband. The plot was particularly special to Dick whose frequent treks up the mountain led him that way. And so it was, that early afternoon, that Alice and Dick stood together for one last time at Charlie's grave, placing lilacs at the foot of his head stone.

Flight 349 from Boston was to arrive at 6:35 p.m. the operator had informed Sean Merrill. Sean's wife, Jean, had prepared the spare room for Alice and had set up a folding bed for Dick as a temporary set up, knowing that Dick would be visiting for only a month or less if Alice found her own place before Dick returned to school. Jean Merrill was much younger than Alice and, at fifty-two, had spent most of her life in the warmer climates of the South. She had met Sean in the early '30s when he moved to Florida and began making deliveries to The Boca Beach Motel, a family business owned by Jean's father. Sean worked for a towel and linen supply company covering the resorts and businesses from West Palm Beach to Pompano. Boca Raton was in between the two more popular cities and was considered quite unknown in the 1930s. Plush resorts were mostly in the Palm Beach area but more and more retirees were moving into the Boca area where real estate prices were less expensive.

Sean had never liked the cold weather and the New Hampshire climate was one he very seldom talked about. He had made his move to Florida and firmly believed that this part of the country, with its beaches and tropical climate, would someday be the retirement haven for many of the country's workforce. Jean's father had seen the growth of the Boca area into the 1940s and had recommended to Sean that he put his money into coastal real estate properties before anything else. "It's just a matter of time, Sean, my boy, before that waterfront property will turn to gold," he would tell Sean. Believing that his advice was wise, Sean began by buying a small beach house and, a few years later, an acre of land on the coastal waterway that flowed for miles between the beach properties and those more inland. Sean believed that this property would be more valuable to boat owners as an alternative to the more expensive costs of keeping boats at a marina. "Why not park your boat at your own dock, in your backyard," he would say.

Sean Merrill had arrived in West Palm Beach in 1935 at the age of forty-six. A bachelor who had never seriously worked at any trade for too long, Sean had seen his move to Florida as a new beginning, an opportunity for him to do something on his own. Sean had even driven a delivery truck for Charlie for a while but never saw himself as a potential business owner. His happy-go-lucky attitude and his carefree love for having a good time left him broke most of the time. He had never met the "right" girl until he met Jean Partridge, a quiet but intelligent desk clerk at her father's motel. Theirs was not a passionate courtship, but one based on admiration for each other's values. They were wed in 1936, Sean at forty-seven and Jean at forty-two.

Apparently, Jean had inherited her father's business sense and they began to accumulate more and more property in the Boca Raton area little by little, while both retaining their respective jobs. Glenn Partridge died in a fishing accident five years later in 1941 and Jean was the sole survivor, Glenn's wife having passed away from cancer before Sean had come on the scene. Sean and Jean Merrill immediately became very wealthy and assumed control of the motel and of her father's estate, valued at $2.5 million.

As years went by, Sean saw the continuing Florida population growth and suggested to Jean that they consider opening a family restaurant on property they owned adjacent to the motel. By the summer of 1945, the restaurant was completed and ready to be opened. Jean would continue to operate the motel while Sean would oversee the restaurant operation. Chefs, waiters, and a restaurant manager were all hired and plans had been made for a grand opening in early August.

Alice was family, Sean pondered as he drove from his home in Boca toward the West Palm Beach airport some thirty minutes away. Sean would offer Alice any position she wanted at the restaurant or none at all if she decided against working once she settled into the area. Sean had the deepest respect for Alice. She had stuck by Charlie all these years, even though, Sean knew, Charlie had seen some rougher times before he became successful. Sean felt that Alice had sort of been cheated by Charlie's sudden death and he was determined to do everything he could to make her life as comfortable as possible, even though Charlie would not be around to share it with her.

Flight 349 from Boston was listed as on time as he entered the small terminal at 6:15 p.m. A short while later, Alice and Dick appeared; both carrying warm smiles as Sean greeted them. The flight had been a long silent one for the two of them. The three hours had given each of them time to reflect on the years in New Hampshire while, at the same time, create visions of anxiety and doubt about what lay ahead in the world of year-round warmth and sunshine.

After having settled in at Sean's home, a four-bedroom sprawling ranch complete with its own boat dock, Dick and Alice slowly began the task of becoming familiarized with not only the area, but the style of living that the residents thrived on. Hospitality abounded throughout the community since the community relied almost totally on catering to its visitors. "Exactly what Alice needs, right now, Dick,"

Sean said as they toured the city. "Your mother has been cooped up so long in her kitchen that she needs to be among smiling faces and people, lots of people."

"I'm not so sure that this isn't too much of a change for her, Uncle Sean. I don't know if mom can all of a sudden just relax and shift gears. It's going to take some time. I don't know if I can leave her at the end of the summer. I'm going to worry about her."

"Don't give it another thought, Dick, your Aunt Jean and I don't have any other relatives and your mom's all we got. We'll see to it that she gets whatever she needs to adjust to this climate. Dick, she's sixty-five years old, she's got to slow down a bit. I'm thinking of asking her to maybe just bake desserts for the restaurant. That should keep her busy just a few hours a day, no more. That way, she can learn to unwind and relax with Jean and me. You've got to make your own life now Dick, your mom too!"

The summer months for Dick were totally different than he had been accustomed to. Sean had loaned him one of his cars to use and Alice did not want Dick working that summer at all. The time he spent walking the beaches or riding the open topped car for hours on end, were times for Dick to think about his future, about the regret he felt at not being on better terms with his father before he died, and about the coming September and going back to school. "If only we could have talked more," Dick pondered, "I never got to tell him how much I loved him." This tormented him that summer in Florida.

"Dick, nice of you to call, how are you and how's your mother?" the excited voice at the other end of the phone blurted.

"I'm fine, Father, how's everything at St. Barnaby's?"

"Well, to tell you the truth, Dick, we've had a good summer with lots of tourists attending Masses on weekends and the community is growing every day. We miss your smiling face, though. What's happening with you in Florida and how's your mom?"

"Mom's fine, really settled into this area and she's gotten used to the hot summers and looking forward to her first warm winter. I think it might bother her, though, around Christmas time without the snow and all."

"Father, do you remember our talk last year about me breaking away from my folks and going off on my own?"

"Sounds to me like you've been doing some soul searching on those Florida beaches. That's pretty hard to do with those lovely young ladies parading around in bathing suits down there. Sure, I remember our talk. What have you come up with?"

"I was wondering, Father, is there someone up there I can talk to about the seminary. I think I'd like to become a priest, Father."

The news to Father Gavin came as no surprise. Although he had deliberately avoided talking to Dick too much about the priesthood, for fear that it might look like he was pushing him in that direction, Father Gavin knew though that Dick's interest in the priesthood was not merely a passing thought. He had recalled himself in similar circumstances some years before he had contemplated going to the seminary in Baltimore to study the priesthood.

"That's a big decision, Dick, are you sure you've really thought this out?" Father Gavin sounded like he was discouraging Dick while, in reality, Dick knew that Father Gavin's concern was due to the seriousness of this decision.

"I must find out, Father, that's all I've thought about since my dad died, and now that mom's doing okay on her own, I've got to think of my own future. After a year at Plymouth, I'm not sure that teaching history is for me."

"Father Romeo Gleason at the St. Ignatius Seminary in Baltimore is the guy you want to talk to, Dick. You'll need a sponsor, too, someone who can support your genuine interest on this. I'll call on your behalf to let him know you'll be in touch."

Dick jotted down the phone number for the seminary and told Father Gavin that he'd let him know how he made out with Father Gleason as soon as he could. A visit to the seminary was customary, Father Gavin had mentioned to Dick, and a brief three-to-five day stay would also be required to acclimate potential postulants in the regimen at the seminary. This preliminary period usually eliminated the majority of the interested young men from pursuing the priesthood any further. Continued pursuit by the remaining candidates was no clear indication that priesthood was imminent, but it was a beginning.

That evening, Dick broke the news to his mother that he would visit St. Ignatius in early August just to see what it would be like.

"I'm not surprised; I've seen it in your eyes since you first became an altar boy. You'll never know if it's what you want to do if you don't go up there to Baltimore and find out."

CHAPTER 6

St. Ignatius Seminary was like a self-contained fortress, a reminder to Dick of the castles and mansions he had heard of and seen pictures of in his history courses in high school and at Plymouth. The huge stone structure stood three stories high and extended several hundred feet across a plush apron of lawn that extended far in front of it, bringing out its unobstructed beauty. As Dick's taxi drove up to the entrance gates leading to this grand façade, he felt a tingling sensation overtaking his entire body. He looked at his watch, 10:00 a.m., right on time for his meeting with Father Gleason before being assigned to a room in the postulant candidates' quarters.

No sooner had the taxi driver placed Dick's suitcase beside him and wished him well, there appeared a tall silver-bearded man in clerical robes with a smile that surely was exactly what Dick needed at that moment. For a brief instant, he had become uncertain as to what he was doing here and was tempted to try to flag down the fleeing taxi while he had the chance.

"Hi, I'm Romie Gleason. Welcome to St. Ignatius. And you would be…?"

"Dick Merrill, Father, from Rumney, New Hampshire, Boca Raton, Florida, I mean…"

"I know what you mean, son; Father Gavin and I had a long talk about your coming and he's told me all about you. Let's get your gear inside and I'll show you around."

The grounds were even prettier behind the building than from the entranceway. There were ball fields, walking trails with young men strolling the grounds, and a pond complete with a gazebo surrounded with benches. Inside the main building, there were two huge parlors for greeting visitors and their parents. There were very ornate tables and racks of literature depicting life as a seminarian and Father Gleason told Dick to read as many as he could during his brief stay in the coming week. The building's main floor had wide hallways lined with statues and religious pictures leading to the double doors of the chapel. As you walked the hallways, you could hear the footsteps echo against the twelve-foot high ceilings from the marble floor below. Dick smiled. As he set foot through the doorway of the chapel, he immediately was besieged with the huge glimmer and radiance of sunshine streaming through the stain-glassed windows extending nearly thirty feet high. This chapel was three times the size of St. Barnaby's Church and the biggest place of worship he had ever seen.

As if some magnetic force drew him forward, Dick found himself headed toward the altar and the accompanying pulpit. When he reached his destination and turned to face the vastness that confronted him, he merely smiled. "How does it feel, Dick? Is it a bit scary, overwhelming?"

"It's magnificent, Father, unlike anything I've ever seen before, it's beautiful."

"Come on, let me introduce you to your roommate; he's been here for two years now, his name is Ed McNeil, I think you'll like him."

The dormitory building was adjacent to the main building and housed all seminarians during their entire stay at St. Ignatius. The odds of keeping the same roommate for all four years, Father Gleason related to Dick, were very slim and rarely did it happen. Many postulants lasted for as much as two years, some only one year and many for less than a year. Ed McNeil already had two roommates; Dick would be the third, if only for a week. If Dick decided to enroll at the seminary following the week's activities that depicted life as a seminarian, both he and Ed McNeil would have to agree to continue as roommates; compatibility was essential because of the rigorous schedule of classes and training involved. It was not uncommon, Father Gleason related as they treaded across the lawn to the dormitory, that roommates who eventually both became ordained into the priesthood continued their friendship for the rest of their lives.

August, 1945, was warm in Baltimore and as the two made their way through the dorm entrance and up the stairs to the third floor, Father Gleason could not help but curse how uncomfortable and hot it was wearing his cassock during this kind of weather. A priest in his mid-fifties, he was definitely the typical picture of a priest who had to always look and dress like one, Roman collar and all, even if it meant undue perspiration and discomfort.

"Ah, three-one-one, here we are. I told Ed you'd be arriving this morning, so he should be in."

"Ya, come on in, the McNeil palace awaits you," the voice sounded at the end of Father Gleason's knock. There stood a towering blond man, wearing a baseball cap, a tee shirt full of holes, a pair of khaki Bermuda shorts and sandals. Clothes were strewn across chairs, the beds, and even the dressers. The room looked like it had been ransacked and ready for the demolition team to finish the job.

"Ed, say hello to Dick Merrill, the fellow I said would be rooming with you this week to see if priesthood training is something he really wants to consider or something that's been on his mind for a while and just needs to be dealt with."

"Dick, nice to meet you. I don't know why Father Gleason is hooking you up with me; I don't have a good track record with roommates. There are those here who even think I'm the cause of new guys changing their minds about becoming a priest. I'm even starting to believe that myself, although I can't imagine why. The Lord sure didn't know what he was getting into when he allowed them to let me in here two years ago, I guess."

Dick had never seen such a messy room. The floor was piled with boxes and the wall had baseball players' pictures all over, and the crucifix, in the midst of these posters, was almost unnoticeable. Ed McNeil could sense the look of concern in Dick's expression as he discreetly noticed his eyes scanning the room he would be calling "home," at least for the next week.

"Sorry about the mess; really, I'm not that bad. I just got back from summer vacation at home and I sort of just threw things around to empty my suitcases and get them out of the way. I'll have this place looking like McNeil's palace in no time. Sit down. Where you from, Dick?"

Father Gleason excused himself as he informed Dick that Ed would take care of settling him in and acquainting him with the schedule for the week. "Thanks, Father," yelled Ed, "I'll take good care of him."

"That's what I'm afraid of," sighed Father Gleason as he shut the door on his way out.

The two seemed to hit it off immediately and Dick was quite comfortable carrying on a conversation with Ed McNeil. McNeil was from Rochester, New York and the son of a film company executive who wasn't too keen on his son's announcement to leave LeMoyne University for the seminary.

* * *

In September of that year, Dick Merrill enrolled as a new seminarian at St. Ignatius and decided to room with Ed McNeil, who, as it turned out, really wasn't the sloppy guy that Dick had first thought he was.

Eddie McNeil and Dick Merrill really got to know each other in Dick's first year at the seminary. It seems, as Dick found out, that Eddie's father wasn't just a big executive for a film company, but its president and a very wealthy man.

Ed McNeil was ordained in June, 1948, and was assigned to a parish in Wisconsin. On that day, Ed was surprised and pleased to see his father attending the ceremony and, while he still had doubts about his son's selection, he respected his determination and apparent love for religious life.

Dick Merrill was ordained three years later and was assigned to a small parish in St. Johnsbury, Vermont, just two hours north of Rumney, his childhood home. Alice, Sean, and Jean all attended the ceremony, as did Father Ed McNeil and Father Gavin, and the Merrills flew back to Florida together where Dick spent the summer before leaving for his new parish in late August.

CHAPTER 7

Paris in the summer is lovely to visit and Father Dick Merrill was thrilled to be there in August 1950, a gift from his Uncle Sean following his ordination. The week's stay at a small hotel included breakfast, but Dick's excursions around the city would be on his own, leaving him to decide what sights he wanted to see. On his first day in Paris, it was no wonder that he asked the hotel concierge about the best way to tour the city and arranged for a tour bus from Le Bourget to pick him up.

Françoise found it easy and interesting talking to Dick and the Quinlans following her brief experience with the tour driver. She had always found American tourists very friendly and their involvement during the war years at liberating France made her quest for knowing more about America that much greater.

"Tell me about the Statue de Liberte in New York and about the winds in Chicago. Do you still have cowboys in the Wild West? What about Miami, the White House, and the movie stars of Hollywood?"

It was one question after another and Dick found himself overwhelmed by this barrage of inquiry from the French girl. He could not help but notice her beautiful blue eyes against a suntanned complexion and the long flowing brown hair with a beret atop that seemed to fit perfectly on her head. Her every motion and bubbly personality captured Dick's attention immediately. Once lunch was over and the tour resumed, now with a much more experienced driver than before, Dick seemed to find himself very much interested and attracted to Françoise's every word and move. His smile met her eyes often during the next several hours of the excursion around Paris and he suddenly flashed a frown as the bus approached his hotel, signaling the end of the tour.

Françoise bid farewell to Dick and other passengers as they disembarked. "Perhaps we can continue our conversation about America at another time," Dick was quick to state, surprising himself at his boldness, a far cry from the shy New Hampshire boy most people knew him for.

"Perhaps, monsieur, perhaps."

Dick had dinner with the Quinlans that evening and they mentioned what a delightful person Françoise had been on the tour. Mrs. Quinlan went so far as to state how it seemed that Françoise was attracted to Dick and wouldn't it be nice if Dick had a chance to see her again sometime during his stay in Paris. Following dinner, the Quinlans excused themselves and bid Dick good night and wished him well during the remainder of the week as the Quinlans were off to Nice and the Riviera the next morning.

There is something empty about being alone in a strange city at night. Although the streets of Paris on a summer night were very inviting and filled with people and cafes, where does one go alone at night? It was probably no strange coincidence that led Dick back to the Café Royal as he strolled through the city that evening. Nightlife in Paris begins at 9:00 p.m. and so it was no surprise to see the restaurant bustling with activity and the sidewalk tables bristling with casual conversation and glasses of wine being lifted throughout. Louis Dupont recognized Dick at once as he entered. Anyone aiding Françoise held an instant place in Louis' memory bank and that afternoon's incident with the inexperienced bus driver was no exception.

"Monsieur Merrill, I believe," Louis stated with a beaming smile. "Are you here for dinner, or are you looking for Françoise?"

"Uh, no, I've already had dinner Mr. Dupont, and I was just walking around on this beautiful night. I did not expect that Françoise would be here, I didn't think I'd even end up here!"

"Henri, be sure that table number five is well-taken care of. That is the police chief's son and his fiancée. We need to stay on the good side of the police, you know," Louis motioned to one of the waiters as he was busily about his duties of running a very busy café.

"I was wondering if Françoise ever did separate walking tours when she was not doing the city bus tours. I don't really know anyone else and there is so much to see."

"I am certain that Françoise on her holidays explores more of Paris, Monsieur Merrill. That is an appetite that she has had since she was a small child before the war. She lives in Paris on her own now and if you wish to call her to ask her, you can telephone her at Madame Gagnon's house where she lives, numereau seven-six-one, three-six-one-seven. Nice to see you again, monsieur, enjoy your stay in Paris." Dick copied the number down and left the café as he gestured goodbye to Louis.

Dick never gave much thought to the time of night it was and, as he found his way back to his hotel, picked up the telephone in his room as he entered. The voice at the other end of the receiver was soft and low, "Madame Gagnon, ici."

"Do you speak English, Madame?"

"Yes, un petit peut," she replied. "How may I help you at this late hour?"

"May I speak to Françoise Dupont, please?"

"No, you may not, monsieur," she answered in a more harsh tone. "It is after ten and Françoise is already to bed in her room, I am certain. I can leave a note for her and she can telephone you tomorrow. She gets up early and is usually gone to work before I am up. Who may I say was calling?"

The following day, Dick headed for an early train to Rome and the Vatican, where the Pope made his weekly Wednesday appearance to the public. As a newly ordained priest, Dick had been afforded an audience with His Holiness along with a small group of clergymen. The audience would be brief and, just as well Dick thought, since he had purchased a round trip ticket back to Paris that same afternoon. It was late in the day when he returned to the hotel and received a message from the desk clerk along with his room key. The message read, "Will stop by the hotel again at 7. Françoise Dupont."

"Hello again, Françoise," said Dick in the lobby of the hotel when she arrived a few minutes later. "Sorry I wasn't here when you came by earlier, but I was in Rome and the Vatican today."

"That is ok, Richard, I had just dropped off some tourists at this hotel this afternoon and had Madame Gagnon's note that you called. How did you enjoy the Vatican?"

"Marvelous. I even saw the Pope with a group of priests in a separate room."

"Oh, you were fortunate, Richard; that does not happen too often unless you are a priest or minister with a special pass."

Unsuspecting that Dick was a priest, Françoise quite simply assumed that Dick, who wore casual clothing, had connections in the Catholic Church to get such a special meeting. At that moment, Dick hesitated in telling Françoise that he was Father Merrill, not just Richard Merrill. It was like he didn't want her to know. His face blushed and he badly fumbled for words to change the conversation, surely looking awkward to Françoise in his indecisiveness. He finally managed to blurt out, "Would you have some time one day from now until Sunday to show me some of your favorite sights? Your father told me that no one in Paris knows the sights better than you. I would, of course, pay you whatever you charge."

"Oh, Richard, there is so much to see. Trying to do it all in one day is not possible. You could only see some of the beautiful places in such a short time. Are you interested in churches, museums, the river, or what?"

"Gosh, I never thought about it, but maybe you're free for dinner tonight and we can put a schedule together?"

"I am free during the day on Friday for the price of twenty dollars. Tonight is not good for dinner. I meet my father and we have dinner at his home with my mother every Wednesday. Perhaps tomorrow night?"

"Tomorrow it is, then, shall I go to Madame Gagnon's house to pick you up?"

"No, I will meet you here and we can go to Le Relais, a short walk from here. You can tell me everything you've already seen in Paris and we will plan the day. Au revoir, Richard."

Like a child about to go on a first date, Dick's heart was beating rapidly and he could do little to hide his excitement as he waved goodbye to Françoise. These were not the feelings of one committing to celibacy, but he could not stop himself from the sheer thought of spending the following evening with this charming and beautiful girl, not to mention the entire day on Friday. He had never felt this way before. Perhaps it was just the natural reaction to Parisian girls he had always heard about.

On Thursday, Dick headed for the Louvre and seemed to wander aimlessly through the maze of the museum, forever glancing at his watch and wondering why the day seemed to be moving at a crawl. As much as he tried to compose himself, the more anxious he became at the thought of dinner that evening with Françoise. Like a kid in a candy store, Dick was reacting wildly to what should have been a mutual desire to highlight the sights of the city, nothing more. Following a light lunch in a café near the museum, Dick headed back to his hotel to shower and shave again before Françoise would arrive later that afternoon. At the hotel, the desk clerk informed Dick that a Mademoiselle Dupont called to say that she would not be at the hotel until six o'clock. She would explain the delay when she arrived.

At 5:30 p.m., Dick was dressed in an open shirt and a sports jacket and was sitting in the reception area of the hotel lobby pretending to read a French newspaper. At 6:15 p.m., an eternity later, Françoise appeared through the main door. Dick's mouth opened and his gaze at Françoise was embarrassing. She wore a beautiful dress with a lace trim at the hem, her golden brown hair accented perfectly under her blue beret. Her face and lines were radiant and her perfume totally mesmerized Dick as if he were in a trance. He did all he could to contain himself and had feelings building inside of him that he had not ever had before. Françoise's smile was genuine as she greeted him with the customary kiss on both cheeks.

"Bonjour, Richard, forgive me for being late. Our bus had motor problems and the tour today took longer to finish than usual. Et bien, shall we go?"

The walk to Le Relais took all of five minutes. Françoise had reserved a table in the far corner of the restaurant so that they could discuss touring plans for Friday. The table was lit by a candle and the amber light was just enough to highlight the radiance of Françoise. The lines of her body were perfect and with each of her moves and gestures, Dick was once again aroused in her presence. Dinner was perfect and when the waiter presented the bill to Dick, Françoise abruptly suggested that they put the final touches to Friday's schedule at Dick's hotel room.

As they strolled back to the hotel, Dick found himself reaching out for her hand and, surprisingly, she accepted this gesture with a slight squeeze of her own hand in his and a warm smile. Her cheeks looked flushed and her eyes were dazzling. Under the lights and the brightly-lit sky of a Parisian night, Francoise was beyond just a pretty face. That night was more than Dick had ever thought about. He found himself in her embrace no sooner than they entered his room. Without pressing his body against hers, he began to very slowly run his hand up and down her body, from where he could feel the rapid beat of her pulse on both sides of her throat, to her chest, her breasts, her stomach, around to one buttock, then down to her thigh. Passion immediately overtook both of them and the young innocence from both of them disappeared quickly as they both experienced love making for the first time. The sound of discovery in her breathing put him over the edge, an though it wasn't simultaneous, a few seconds later she lifted her head and buried her face in his shoulders, holding him tightly. They clutched each other it seemed for hours but, in reality, was a short time. Suddenly, as if the clock had struck the bewitching hour, Françoise dressed quickly and, as she made her way to the door, shouted, "Madame Gagnon will be worried if she doesn't hear me coming home, she's like my mother away from home. A demain, Richard."

There was so much mixed emotion that faced Dick as he realized what he had just done. He had not yet been a priest a month and had succumbed to his vow of celibacy in a moment of passion. What would he do now, who would he tell, who would understand this human frailty? He could not see Françoise the next morning, he thought, yet would she feel betrayed if he appeared in the lobby dressed as a priest for the day's activities? What was he to do?

That night seemed endless as he tossed and turned trying to decide how he would face Françoise the next day. With the early morning light shining through his window at dawn, Dick had decided to continue the charade for this one day. What harm could it do? He would be heading back to Florida in a few days and then to his new parish in Vermont anyway.

Françoise was alive and warm when she greeted Dick at 9:00 a.m. Dick found her as beautiful as the night before. The day touring Paris was unlike any he had ever been through before. What originally was to be a guided tour through the best places in Paris ended up being a lovers' day holding hands at every opportunity. They made love again that night and planned on meeting again for dinner at Le Relais on Saturday night at 7:00 p.m.

Dick was scheduled to return home on a Monday morning flight from Le Bourget. Although Françoise knew this, she shrugged it from her mind and all she could think about was seeing Dick again on Saturday.

The great deception. That's all that Dick could think about. Not only had he violated his vows but he had also deceived an innocent young woman by misleading her into thinking that this was an acceptable young love affair that would merely end soon. He could not leave it at that, nor did he want to hurt Françoise, but, she would get over this in time and go on with her life, he thought, and better for her to know the truth.

At 7:00 p.m., as she entered Le Relais, Dick was sitting at the same table where they sat the first night. The dim lighting allowed Françoise to see Dick's face, but she did not focus on anything else as she approached him. Suddenly, she noticed more as the light unveiled more as he sat dressed in black with his Roman collar on. Françoise became hysterical and shouted out loud, "Richard, Richard, qu'est ce que sait? You are a priest, a priest? How could you do this to me, how could you let me do this," she screamed. She broke down in tears and bolted out of the restaurant and all that Dick could do was sit there, speechless and teary-eyed himself.

On Monday morning, Dick was on a plane back to Boca. The plane ride gave Dick the time to himself that he needed to sort this all out. He would write to Françoise and hoped that she would understand his position and not think harshly of him and their abrupt departure. She deserved some explanation; she deserved at least that much.

CHAPTER 8

"My dearest Françoise," began the letter that Dick had carefully composed in early September 1950 while experiencing one of his first peaceful moments since arriving at St. Catherine's Church in St. Johnsbury, Vermont. "I hope this letter reaches you and that you are well. Forgive me for not having said goodbye to you before I left Paris and for not telling you in the beginning that I was a newly ordained priest. I was and still am very fond of you and I cherish our time together. It is something I will never forget. I wish you a wonderful life and career in Paris and sincerely hope that you find a wonderful man to share it with. Know that you will always be in my prayers and, should you ever truly need my assistance for anything, at any time, you can write to me at this address. Even if I am no longer assigned at St. Catherine's, the letter will be forwarded to me wherever I may be." The letter was signed Father Richard Merrill and addressed to Mlle. Françoise Dupont, c/o Madame Henriette Gagnon, 171 rue Madeleine, Paris, France.

August quickly turned to September and October as Dick began to become accustomed with the role of a parish priest. His personality and warmth were well received among the parishioners and his youthfulness and exuberance were evident in his weekly sermons when compared to the more serious and mundane sermons given by the pastor at St. Catherine's, Father Michael O'Malley.

Things were not going as well, however, in Paris. Françoise was pregnant. She was ashamed to announce this to her parents. They were finally leading a more comfortable and relaxed lifestyle now that the Dupont children were all off on their own, Françoise having been the last to leave the nest. When she called in sick several times at the tour company, Madame Gagnon became both concerned and suspicious. Françoise finally confided in her and Madame Gagnon was there to console her in these trying times.

"I am too young to raise a child," Françoise tearfully told Madame Gagnon, "and I will not raise a child without a father. My own father would be so disappointed in me if he knew that I was with a child. He must never know."

Madame Gagnon comforted Françoise during the months that followed and it was decided by Françoise that, once the child was born, the baby would be placed for adoption with the Sisters of Mercy Orphanage north of Paris in Giverny.

As the months passed, Françoise visited her parents less frequently as her pregnancy began to show, no matter how loosely she wore her clothing. In April, she called her mother to tell her that the tour company was sending her outside the city to establish tours beyond the city of Paris. She asked her mother to pass on the news to her father, as she would be leaving immediately the following morning. She would call them as often as she could during her absence and assured them that she would be fine in her upcoming travels. For the first time in her life, Françoise had lied to her parents and she cried that evening at the thought of having done so, but the disgrace of having a child out of wedlock in a very Catholic city like Paris would have brought shame on the family. A twenty-year-old girl just didn't do this.

Madame Gagnon had planned to handle the birth discreetly by bringing in an old friend and midwife in early May of that year. As her delivery neared, Françoise could hardly walk, her stomach unusually large, or so Madame Gagnon thought. Once the contractions began and her water broke, the midwife was summoned immediately. At the first sight of Françoise, the midwife stated that this would be a very large baby.

Françoise delivered twin boys. The delivery became so difficult for the midwife that she needed Madame Gagnon's doctor to help in the delivery, which was something they were hoping to avoid. Doctor Jean-Louis Mathieu was troubled following the birth of the twin boys. He determined a short while later that it would be quite dangerous if Françoise attempted to have more children in the future because she had lost quite a lot of blood from hemorrhaging. When he related this to Françoise, she did not fully focus on the long-term implications and was only too glad to have this ordeal over with.

The boys were named Charles Andre and Robert Conrad. Within the month, she would turn them over to the orphanage in Giverny for adoption. She swore Madame Gagnon to secrecy about the boys' birth and the eventual trip to the orphanage. For the entire month of June, Françoise was depressed at these events and knew that she had not communicated with her parents since just before the delivery. She had left the employ of the tour company when she had lied to her parents about the assignment outside of Paris. Now, she was faced with the need to find another job, to pick up the pieces of her life and go on, something she had not needed to do before.

Claude Gagnon did not visit his older sister often because his director duties at the Louvre kept him so preoccupied that he had little time to spend with his own wife and children. Nevertheless, in early July, Claude stopped in on Henriette Gagnon for lunch and to catch up on his sister's health, not having been there since her husband had passed away nearly two years before. Henriette's children were all grown and on their own living in southern France, along the coast of Nice, and all three worked for a resort hotel in that area. None of the children, two girls and one boy, were married yet and Henriette knew of no upcoming nuptials. They all seemed happy and doing well in the warmer climate as compared to the colder winter months of Paris.

Henriette was a woman of meager needs and the income she earned from renting her three apartments was sufficient for her to live on. Claude, nonetheless, worried about how long his elderly sister could continue to manage the household. She was now in her early sixties and her hearing and eyesight were beginning to fail. It was on this day that Claude met Françoise for the first time. She was with Henriette when he arrived and was busily doing some housework and about to do some of the washing when Henriette asked her to join them for lunch. Henriette raved about Françoise's knowledge of French history and sites, citing her rapid rise in the local tour business. What a coincidence, he thought, as the Louvre seriously considered beginning gallery tours as the tourist traffic became increasingly hard to manage. It was also evident that more and more tourists were interested in guided explanations of the assorted artwork in the museum.

"Mademoiselle Dupont, the museum is planning on beginning museum tours soon, and I was wondering if you would be interested in taking on a new position. My sister tells me that you have been conducting bus tours in and around Paris for a few years and that you are comfortable doing such tours." This would be a fresh start, she thought, and did not hesitate to accept the position.

The Louvre had apparently just hired its first guided tour leader. Madame Gagnon was pleased that her brother was in such a position and that he would be there to keep a watchful eye on Françoise. Life would begin again for Françoise.

CHAPTER 9

"This letter was hand-delivered to me last week. The man delivering it would not give it to me until he was certain that I was Father Richard Merrill," Father Dick related to Jim Howard.

> *Mon cher Richard,*
>
> *It has been over thirty-five years since we have communicated to each other, and this letter is very difficult for me to write to you. Since you had decided to remain as a priest, I did not want to complicate your life with mine; we were so far apart from each other. My life has been good since I left Paris in 1955 and married Amhad Maurier who, at the time, was the Crown Prince and next heir to the throne of the small country of Khatamori, a country rich in oil north of Saudi Arabia. Amhad and I were not blessed with children and now that he is older, he worries*

that he will have no heir to the throne that he inherited following his father's death in 1965. He is seventy now and has trouble with his kidneys. We have the finest doctors looking at him but there is only so much they can do.

Khatamori has a law that any child of the monarch is eligible to inherit the throne. The child does not need to be from our marriage, he can be from a previous marriage, his or mine. The law here states that when two people marry, their family becomes as one, including children that come from either the man or the wife, even though such children were not from a marriage. Amhad and I have been married but once and to each other. You are most certainly wondering why I am telling you all of this when we have been apart for so long.

Richard, you were my first experience in lovemaking, and I will remember that forever. A few months after you returned to America, I found that I was with your child. You must understand that this is very bad for a young Catholic girl in France since we were not married. On May 9, 1951, our twin sons were born and I named them Charles and Robert. I had not worked for several months before the babies and could not raise them myself. I sent them to the Orphanage of the Sisters of Mercy in Giverny. Soon they were adopted to separate families and, over the years, I have kept in contact with the orphanage and had them send money from me to their parents. But I do not know where they live and what their last names are. They would be thirty-six years of age today.

There is trouble I fear, and I must ask you to help. General Answa Talon is the head of the military here in Khatamori and that is but like a police chief to regulate violators of our country's laws, mostly small crimes.

Since Amhad's ill health, Talon has begun an investigation to verify that there are no living heirs to the throne, a position that he will get if there are no children to succeed Ahmad. I am not certain if he knows about Charles and Robert, but if he does, he will surely do anything to kill them before allowing either of them to accept their rightful place in my kingdom. I am forbidden from leaving the country without Amhad, that is the law, and I have sent this letter to you in the hands of my most trusted servant.

Richard, I should have told you about the boys years ago, but did not want you to worry about them or me. I do not know what you can do but any help is needed. I fear Amhad may not live until June of the coming year, so I have been told.

Françoise

"I need you to find my sons, Mr. Howard," blurted Father Dick. "I need to be sure they are safe and remain safe but I don't have a clue how to do this and, at my age, I can't move around like I used to. I've saved over one hundred thousand dollars and I can get more from an old trust fund my mother had set up for me years ago. Can you help?"

Jim Howard had lived a strange life since being discharged from the Army following Vietnam. For a short time, he had served with the CIA as an undercover agent in Europe keeping tabs on Russian activity in the area just after the Bay of Pigs incident and Cuban blockade. His CIA service, combined with his former military years was enough for him to take a government pension in 1985. Bored to death, he took to selling insurance just to keep himself busy. Howard had never married and the steel plate in his right leg, a reminder of Vietnam, kept him from doing much more, even at the young age of forty-five.

"What exactly do you want to do once someone finds them, Father, or at least finds out where they live?"

"I'll figure that out when they're found. Right now, I need to find them first."

"Let me see what I can do, Father, and I'll get back to you."

Howard still had contacts in Europe who, when they left the military together and did operative work, could be trusted to do this, and some of these contacts were in France. Jim left the rectory and informed Father Dick that he would know pretty quickly if his contacts were still active and what the cost would be to locate them. Jim indicated that there wasn't much he could do beyond that.

Father Dick thanked Howard for his time and asked him to not use his name with any of his contacts; they had no need to know whom the request came from.

Two days later, Father Dick answered the phone at the rectory, "Ten thousand plus expenses to locate them, and twenty thousand will give you their life history. Father, that's for each boy—twenty thousand up front and the rest when I get the report from my man in Europe." Jim Howard had drawn on an old favor from a former Army buddy who worked for the American embassy in Paris. Since the government prohibited embassy employees from having side jobs, Jim merely told Father Dick that the assignment had been taken by a good reliable contact in Europe. The money was wired that afternoon and news of any progress would be faxed to Jim as quickly as possible. The starting point would be the orphanage.

The two-story orphanage housed one hundred and twenty children of all ages, from a nursery with infants, all the way to a few teenagers, with the older ones having supervisory duties of some of the younger ones since there were not enough nuns to handle such a large number of children by themselves. While the stone building looked quite old and in need of repair, the interior facility was kept in spotless condition. Karl Pelland's appointment with Sister Marie-Louise Laliberte was for 2:00 p.m. and Karl was right on time. She greeted the visitor warmly and, after being seated in her small but tidy office, asked the nature of his visit.

"That is out of the question, monsieur; we do not give out such information. We must respect and protect the names of the women who have left babies here over the years. We cannot and have not done this before and will not do so now. If that is all, then I bid you good-bye monsieur."

Exactly what he expected to hear. Karl, however, did not rise from his chair upon hearing this news from Sister Marie-Louise; instead he asked to be heard.

"Are you familiar with the name of Françoise Dupont, Sister?"

"No, monsieur, I am not. Why do you ask?"

"What about the Princess of Khatamori?"

"No, monsieur."

"May I ask how long you have been the Superieur at the orphanage, Sister?"

"Since just after the war, in the early 1950s, monsieur, and many children have come through this orphanage and have gone on to live very happy lives."

"It must be difficult to run such a large place with mostly donations from the people in the area, Sister.

Do you often get other money from wealthy people who perhaps were once orphans themselves?"

"But of course, monsieur; we grow much of our own food from the gardens, but that is not enough. We need clothes and other things for the children. Why do you ask?"

Karl could see that this questioning was upsetting the good sister.

"For nearly twenty years, you received money from the princess to be forwarded to the parents of two adopted boys from this orphanage. In return, the princess included an additional tidy amount for use by the orphanage, is that not so?"

"How do you know this, monsieur, and why are you seeking these children?"

"Did you not get all this money from the princess every year for all this time?"

"Yes, monsieur, from the Princess Farah, and yes it was for two boys named Charles and Robert. I never knew why she sent the money for these boys; she was not the mother to my knowledge. Unless, oh mon dieu, unless the princess was not always a princess. What is this all about?"

"Nothing to be alarmed about, Sister. The princess has sent me here to bring you a final gift of five thousand dollars for all your kindness over the years," Karl announced as he produced a banker's check from the Banc Nationale de Paris made out to the Sisters of Mercy. "All that she asks in return is the names of the two couples who adopted the two boys and the latest address you have for them. The princess wants to send the parents more money as she is getting old and had promised the boys' mother that she would always take care of them. I am sure you can understand the need for the addresses, Sister."

"I don't know, monsieur, this is highly unusual, but the Princess Farah has been so generous to us, we even have named our Jardin de Farah flower gardens after her and the children's dining area is now Farah Hall."

"Will you deny this wonderful lady the chance to do more good for the boys and for the orphanage?" Sister Marie's eyes never left sight of Karl's hand holding the check where she could plainly see its amount and who it was made payable to.

"The records are old, monsieur, and I do not know exactly when these boys came here. I do not believe we still have this information; it has not been for fifteen years or so since we heard from the Princess Farah."

"May, 1951, Sister, Charles Andre and Robert Conrad."

Sister Marie-Louise asked Karl to accompany her to a basement file room where an old folder was kept listing all entrants to the orphanage by their date of admission. Next to each name were the names and addresses of adoptive parents, the date of the adoption, and the natural mother and father's names, if they had been given.

"May 23, 1951, here it is, monsieur, the two children's names and their mother's name, Françoise Dupont. I wonder how the Princess Farah knew Mademoiselle Dupont?"

"I really don't know, Sister. What are the names of the adopting parents?"

"Jean-Paul et Catherine Larouche, twenty-three rue Bernier, Chartres, for Charles Andre and Carl and Judy Elliott, 5 boulevard des Agneaux, Paris."

Karl presented the check to Sister Marie-Louise and thanked her for her assistance. The first step in finding the sons of Father Dick had just been taken. The journey was far from over.

Twenty-three rue Bernier in Chartres was an apartment house with four apartments. The owner had purchased the property in 1965. All four units were large five-room flats that served as quality residences for executives working in Paris and wanting to live on a quieter street in the suburbs. The owner was not familiar with the Larouche family but mentioned to Karl that one of the tenants had lived there since the early 1950s and, perhaps, he could help. Karl's persistence paid off as the long-time resident did indeed remember Jean-Claude Larouche as an interpreter for the American Red Cross office in Paris. They had bought a house in Chartres some years ago but that he had lost touch with them. He suggested to Karl that he try the Red Cross office, which was still located in Paris. Instead, Karl's visit to the town hall produced records that indicated that the Larouches had purchased property on rue St. Jean in 1965 and there were no records indicating any sale of the property since then.

"Madame Larouche, my name is Karl Pelland from the American embassy in Paris. Is your son Charles at home?"

"Charles does not live here anymore, monsieur, may I ask what this is about?"

"Yes, of course, madam, but it would be best if I could explain to both you and your husband, Jean-Claude, I believe."

"Jean-Claude passed away two years ago, monsieur, and I live alone now that Charles has moved to Dijon. But why are you looking for Charles?"

"Madame, forgive me for being so bold, but does Charles know that he once lived in the orphanage in

Giverny? It appears that he has been left money from a woman who claims to be his real mother. Have you ever told Charles that he was adopted by you in 1951?"

Obviously surprised to hear the news in such a sudden manner, Catherine Larouche, a woman in her early sixties, immediately became defensive as her expression revealed the unexpected announcement she had dreaded to hear for years. It was not that the Larouches had not told Charles of his origin when he was a teenager, it was the news that his birth mother, who had abandoned him, suddenly wanted to now enter his life, a woman who, she feared, would steal the affection of the only living being still close to her.

"My son knows that we adopted him when he was an infant, barely a month old, but the orphanage does not reveal the name of the mother if that is the mother's wish. Charles had tried to find out her name, something he wanted to know, but never was able to."

"I need to speak with Charles, madam. May I have his address or do I need to find out some other way where in Dijon he lives? The mother does not live in France, madam, and I do not believe she has an interest in interfering with Charles's life, merely to leave him some inheritance when she dies. I cannot tell you her name, but I do know that she is quite wealthy now. I have just been asked to verify his whereabouts."

Charles Andre Larouche was a history professor at the Universite de Bourgogne in Dijon, single, and a blond-haired six-footer, nothing like his adoptive parents who were both of much smaller stature. Karl headed for Dijon that afternoon.

It was late when he arrived in Dijon so he decided to check in to a hotel, enjoy dinner and a glass of wine, and get to bed early for a fresh start in the morning. But first, before he got too comfortable, Karl sent a fax to Jim Howard updating him on his progress and his next steps. Once the status of Charles Larouche was assured, he would focus his attention on beginning the search for Robert Elliott.

Dinner at the hotel was at 7:00 p.m. Karl's fax had gone off by 6:15p.m. This gave Karl time to relax in the hotel lounge with a pre-dinner glass of brandy, just the thing on a cold early November day. The lounge was very typical of tastefully decorated lounges in a quiet hotel in France. Large stuffed Queen Anne chairs by a fireplace were ideal for unwinding over an aperitif and catching up on the news of the day from the assortment of newspapers neatly arranged on a corner credenza. Karl's brandy arrived almost immediately once ordered and he reached for the afternoon edition of the local newspaper, Le Bien Public. In the lower right hand of the front page were the following headlines:

UNIVERSITY PROFESSOR FOUND DEAD AT HOME

At 9:00 a.m. this morning, a colleague found the body of Charles Andre Larouche, a professor of history at the Universite de Bourgogne. The colleague, Prof. Jean Marchand, was meeting Prof. Larouche at his flat where the two were working on an upcoming seminar they were presenting later this month at the college. The police arrived at the scene to find the professor's flat in a shambles, the obvious result of a struggle. Professor Larouche suffered from a blow to the head from a blunt instrument thought to be a fireplace poker found nearby. The police have sealed the flat while attempting to amass more information from the crime scene. They were not aware of any motive for the professor's death which could have resulted from a conflict following the intrusion by an assailant on the professor. Professor Larouche, 36, was single and is survived by his mother, Catherine Larouche of Paris who has been notified of the professor's death. A suspect is being sought based on a description given to the Paris authorities by Madam Larouche of an individual earlier today seeking her son's address.

Karl gasped as he read the story. Madam Larouche would remember his face and name. Why had he said he was from the American embassy in Paris, which is where he really worked? Surely the police would go there and figure out from photographs what Karl Pelland looked like. What kind of assignment had Jim Howard given him, what the hell was going on here?

CHAPTER 10

The phone rang at Jim Howard's apartment in Providence. It was one o'clock in the morning and Jim was quite groggy when he answered.

"Jim, what the hell are you doing to me, what mess have you gotten me into?" Karl shouted over the receiver from the telephone vestibule of the hotel.

"Who is this, Karl, is that you, Karl? This better be important, do you know what time it is here? I got your fax a little while ago, sounds like good progress."

"Forget the fax, you asshole, the kid is dead, he was murdered this morning, it's all over the front page here in Dijon, and I'm the only guy they're looking for right now. The mother gave the Paris police my description. I didn't see any reason not to tell her about the American embassy in case she needed to contact me with more information later on, but, shit man, I never expected her to give this out."

"Calm down, Karl, you didn't do anything wrong. From the time you left Mrs. Larouche's house to the time you checked into the hotel will surely show that you were on the road from Paris to Dijon all that time."

"How the hell do I know when this guy was knocked off, the paper just said that they found his body at nine a.m. this morning, not how long he had been dead. What's going on here, you son of a bitch, what the hell have you gotten me into?"

"Karl, I didn't expect anything to happen, only that you would trace the whereabouts of the two kids. Can't the embassy vouch for you being there yesterday or last night as well? If you can account for your time, you'll be eliminated quickly as a suspect. But if they question you, Karl, tell them the truth, that I hired you to find the kid."

Before the conversation continued, Karl noticed two gendarmes standing outside the phone booth giving him the once over. "Gotta go, Jim, I'll call you back as soon as I can."

The car registered to Karl Pelland, a silver 1986 Audi, had been spotted in the hotel lot. The Paris police had wired this information, along with the license plate, to the Dijon police as soon as Madam Larouche mentioned Karl's name. Karl had some explaining to do.

At the local police station, Karl explained his visit to Madam Larouche earlier that morning, mentioning that he had been asked to find the location of two orphans. He also mentioned how he came to get Madam Larouche's address and the nun from the orphanage. And why would he give his real name if he was going to commit a crime.

Fortunately for Karl, two co-workers accounted for him the night before at an embassy social, making it nearly impossible for him to drive to Dijon that evening and be back to meet Madam Larouche the following morning in Paris. For now, he was free to go but was asked to be available for further questioning through his address at the embassy. Ironically, Karl was asked if he knew of any reason someone would want to harm Charles Larouche, to which he honestly answered no. Jim Howard had not seen the need to divulge any danger to the twins.

"Jim, I'm off the hook for now but I may be in a mess back at the office when I explain all of this to my boss. I'm sure he'll want to know what I was doing here in Dijon. As far as you and I are concerned, Jim, this was just a favor, understand, I never got paid anything to do this, agree?"

"Agree."

"Do you still want me to find the other kid? Is he in danger too? What aren't you telling me, good buddy?" Karl muttered sarcastically.

"Just let me tell you this, Karl, if you don't find this other twin, Robert Elliott, before someone else does, he might wind up dead too. That's all I can tell you right now, but the kid may be a target and has no idea why. Find him fast, Karl, please, it's really important. I'll explain more later, but just find him!"

"Okay, okay, Jim, but I'll need more money. Something tells me that finding this Robert Elliott may not be so easy. I'm heading back to Paris in the morning. Wire another ten thousand to the same place as before. You're going to owe me, big time, Howard, big time."

"Yeah, I know."

CHAPTER 11

In July 1951 the Musee du Louvre was attracting many visitors. The Louvre was the national art museum of France and occupied the site of a thirteenth century fortress. The building of the Louvre was started in 1546 during the reign of Francis I, according to the plans of the French architect Pierre Lescot. Additions were made to the structure during the reigns of almost every subsequent French monarch. The structure, which until 1682 was a residence for the kings of France, is one of the largest palaces in the world. By the mid-nineteenth century the vast complex was completed, covering more than forty-eight acres, and is a masterpiece of architectural design and sculptural adornment.

The nucleus of the Louvre collections is the group of Italian Renaissance paintings, among them several by Leonardo da Vinci. Over the years that the museum had been open to the public, the holdings were significantly enriched by acquisitions made for the monarchy by several cardinals and by Napoleon. Among its greatest treasures were two of the most famous sculptures of the ancient world: the Victory of Samothrace, Venus de Milo, and Leonardo's famous portrait, Mona Lisa.

During the war in the 1940s, protection of all of the Louvre's priceless masterpieces was effected by their removal to secret depositories outside Paris. Claude Gagnon had been instrumental in the movement of much of the artwork outside of Paris and, once the war had ended, he had been appointed one of the seven curatorial positions at the museum. In 1950, Claude was elevated to the position of Directeur Generale at the Louvre, the highest position in the museum.

Françoise was added to the Department of Paintings, considered by many scholars the most important in the world, and including several thousand works of the various European schools. Its enormous collection of French paintings ranged from the Middle Ages to the early nineteenth century. Françoise was to spend nearly a month becoming familiar with each painting in the gallery in preparation for the first guided gallery tour set to begin in August of that year.

As a result of her exposure to dealing with tourists and other local visitors to the Paris area during her stay with the bus tour company, Françoise was a natural in cheerily escorting groups through the vast art collections in her area. Claude was very watchful of Françoise and the progress she made in understanding the history of the old masters and their works. His sister Henriette had now passed on the watchful eye duties of Françoise to Claude and, as the years passed, Claude could only hope that someday his own daughter would end up like Francoise.

By 1956, Françoise had been elevated to the position of Director of the Department of Paintings and had assumed much greater responsibilities than she could have imagined. Her parents visited her often but the vastness of the galleries tended to tire them easily each time they came. Françoise could see the weariness in her father's eyes, but he always glowed in her presence.

Ahmad Maurier was the only son of King Fatam of Khatamori. Throughout his young life, Ahmad had been educated not only in the ways of his country, but also in the history of western civilizations and customs. King Fatam believed strongly that it was important to understand the ways of other cultures of the world if you planned on dealing with those nations. Khatamori, as an oil-rich country, sold much oil to European countries. Amhad, now aged thirty-nine and still unmarried, was continuing his education of European culture by agreeing to evaluate the king's own art collection at the palace in Banra. In his own mind, Ahmad did not see the merits of knowing the real value of such artwork since the king could buy whatever artwork he chose to regardless of price. To appease his father, however, Ahmad agreed to a month-long journey to the Louvre in Paris where Claude Gagnon would assist Ahmad in evaluating techniques of artwork. Claude had asked Françoise to assist him in the several private audiences granted to Ahmad for tutoring at the museum, all for a hefty price to the museum, of course. Additionally, in view of Françoise's extensive knowledge of Parisian sites, Claude had offered the museum's assistance to the prince to include landmarks within Paris. Since Françoise was in charge of the Louvre's painting displays, coupled with her touring capabilities, she was the natural choice for the task, in Claude's mind.

Prince Ahmad arrived with his entourage at Le Bourse airport on a Sunday afternoon in late May. Later that day, Françoise arrived at Hotel Marseilles and knocked on the door of Room 500. As no surprise to her, the prince had rented half of the fifth floor of the hotel, including his own personal suite of four adjoining rooms. A tall very dark man answered the door. He was richly dressed in robes and wore a turban on his head. The man wore several gold rings on his fingers.

"How may I help you?"

"Bonjour, I am Françoise Dupont of the Louvre and I am here representing the museum to personally welcome his highness to Paris." As Françoise entered the foyer to the suite, the servant immediately took notice that Françoise was not wearing a hat or a veil on her head or face.

"You cannot meet with the prince in this manner, madame. All women speaking to the prince must be shielded in the face and head. I will get you the proper clothing before introducing you to Prince Ahmad."

"That will not be necessary, monsieur, as I will not wear a veil or a hat unless I choose to. That is not the custom here in Paris, or in France for that matter, and women certainly do not hide their faces for anyone. And besides, if I am to tutor the prince at the Louvre for the next few weeks and also show him around the streets of Paris, I most certainly will not do so in disguise. Please tell that to the prince."

The servant asked Françoise to wait in the foyer, and he soon disappeared behind double-sliding doors into a gigantic living area of sofas and chairs against a backdrop of several large glass doors leading to a balcony overlooking the city.

Several minutes went by, and Françoise started reconsidering whether her reply had sounded ruder than it had been intended to be. Surely the prince at the earliest opportunity would inform Claude of this behavior, she thought.

"Madame Dupont, the prince will see you now," came a loud announcement as the doors slid open.

"It is Mademoiselle Dupont, monsieur, not madame."

"Forgive me, mademoiselle, and thank you for correcting me."

"Your Highness, may I present Mademoiselle Françoise Dupont from the Louvre."

The living area must have been thirty feet long and nearly as wide as the majestically dressed man began his approach toward Françoise. He was dressed head-to-toe in a silk robe with glowing crystals attached throughout. He also had several huge rings on his fingers and a richly decorated turban with a sapphire stone in the forehead section. He was lighter skinned than the servant, with shiny dark eyes and a broad smile that unveiled stunningly white teeth against his darker complexion. Prince Ahmad was a very handsome man, a feature that Françoise noticed immediately.

"Ah, Mademoiselle Dupont, please forgive me for the earlier formality by my servant, he is accustomed to such protocol for visitors to the palace in Banra."

"That is quite all right, Your Highness, my comments to him were not intended to be insulting to your customs, but to merely inform him that we do not do this in France, regardless of who the visitor is. Welcome to Paris. I trust that your hotel accommodations are suitable."

"Quite comfortable, thank you. Although, I must confess to not having seen your city from the terrace yet. Shall we do that now, mademoiselle, over some tea perhaps?"

"That would be wonderful, Your Highness, and perhaps I can point out a few of Paris's well-known sights for you."

As the two entered the marble-tiled terrace, complete with ornate serving tables and gothic sculptured chairs, Françoise was taken over by the prince's charm and awareness of European custom. As they approached the terrace railing, the prince began to untangle his turban as if he was removing it. The process puzzled Françoise until, at last, Prince Ahmad stood before her with his perfectly combed black hair, slicked back in a glimmer.

"I have noticed that most gentlemen in your country do not wear anything on their heads. I will do the same while I am here. Please, sit down, mademoiselle."

"I do not wish to draw attention to myself."

Françoise could not help but wonder why such a man with so much power and education was a bachelor. Surely, he must be a womanizer, she thought. And, likely, he had had his choice of many women in Khatamori and had found no need to marry yet. Perhaps it was customary to have several wives in his country, Françoise pondered.

"Forgive me for saying, mademoiselle, but you appear to be so young to have such an important position at the Louvre," Prince Ahmad inquired. "How is this to be?"

Françoise related her childhood experiences with her father's tutelage and the subsequent tour business, all of which led to the opportunity to conduct museum tours at the Louvre. The prince was fascinated by her enthusiasm and good nature. He could not help but gaze at her as she went on and on, a trait she had acquired in the museum over the years.

"You will call me Ahmad during my stay here in Paris, so as not to draw any attention to me, something I do not need."

"And then, you may call me Françoise, Monsieur Ahmad."

"If you don't mind also, I will wear French clothing for our visits at the museum and throughout Paris. Again, I do not want for people to be looking at me because of the way I dress."

"Do you require some assistance in getting new clothing, or have you already taken care of that?"

"No, uh, Françoise, I have all the necessary items. The robes you see me in now will only be worn while I am here in my private quarters. And now if you will excuse me, Françoise, I am weary from my journey and need to rest. Perhaps you will join me here later this evening for dinner, as my guest."

"Oh, I am sorry, Ahmad, but I have made other plans for the evening. Should I meet you here in the morning or will you go directly to the Louvre to begin our instruction?" Françoise inquired, embarrassed.

"At the museum would be fine, Françoise. Shall we say around nine a.m.? Until then, I hope your evening is pleasant."

As they walked through the hotel suite, Françoise was engulfed with the smell of incense throughout, a very refreshing fragrance that she was not familiar with.

"Oh, what a wonderful smell this is, is that from your country, Ahmad?"

"Yes, we light such burning candles as a spiritual request to Allah to bless these rooms we occupy. It is again a custom which I will keep within these quarters, although I must admit that, in my country we might take this for granted since it is used everywhere. There is even a liquid fragrance used by Khatamori women that is very similar to this one."

"What is it called?"

"It is called the *Flower of Heaven* to represent the aroma of flowers and the respect that these things are all gifts from Allah."

Françoise bid goodbye to the prince and headed for the elevators leading her down to the lobby. Fool, she thought. Why did I tell him I had other plans tonight when I had no such thing? Just as well, she mumbled to herself. She could use the relaxing evening in anticipation of some likely hectic days ahead. Nevertheless, there was something about Ahmad Maurier that gave her a strange feeling inside, something she had not felt toward anyone for many years. Perhaps it was this feeling that made her hesitate at Ahmad's invitation, a cautious denial of preventing such feelings from surfacing further.

On Monday, Françoise was at the museum at 7:00 a.m., the normal start of her day. She would review the schedule of tours for the day. She no longer did many museum tours herself but would arrange the assignment of tours to others, carefully matching the tour leader to the group. Some of her staff was better with school groups while others were more fluent in other languages that accommodated various groups from outside of France. The tours ran several hours and overlapped, beginning in different parts of the museum to avoid congestion in any one gallery.

Françoise had developed this system to maximize the flow of traffic in the galleries and Claude had been remarkably impressed with her ability to create this system.

Promptly at 9:00 a.m., Ahmad arrived at the Louvre, strikingly handsome in a gray suit, complete with silk tie and matching handkerchief in the breast pocket; his hair combed precisely the same as he had uncovered the afternoon earlier. His shoes were polished and appeared to be right out of the shoe box. Françoise had failed to alert Ahmad to the amount of walking involved in gallery tours and Parisian sightseeing and she could only imagine how sore his feet would be at the end of the day. She made a point to suggest to him that, on future days, he should consider more comfortable attire, less formal, and a pair of shoes or sandals that would be less strenuous on his feet. Ahmad laughed at the suggestion, commenting that there was no such thing as a prince in casual attire when in public view. Customs were sacred to such royalty, whether in Khatamori or elsewhere. He did, however, reserve judgment on wearing different shoes pending the outcome of his first day's adventures.

The Louvre museum houses more than six thousand European paintings dating from the end of the thirteenth century to the mid-nineteenth century, from miniatures to monumental canvases. The Department of Paintings was organized into national schools, subdivided by country and within century from particular countries for France and Italy. Additional countries represented include Spain, Germany, the Netherlands, Flanders, Holland, and Great Britain. All of the paintings were located on the first and second floors of the museum.

Françoise began her instructions in the museum area covering French artists during the fifteenth century.

Each artist had a different style and flare for varying details and the use of color. Françoise was careful to point this out to Ahmad as they began what would surely be a lengthy set of informative meetings for four days each week over the next month. The fifth day would be spent touring the city with Saturdays and Sundays left for Ahmad to do as he wished. Evening meetings were not required but left to the discretion of Françoise, Claude, and Ahmad.

Amhad was very quick to learn the differences among the various artists of France and also of the other European countries represented at the museum. On the few occasions that Claude personally took charge of the tutoring, Ahmad showed less enthusiasm. He had grown accustomed to Françoise's open personality, her wit, and her beauty. When compared to the darker skinned women of his country, Françoise's blue eyes and brown hair nicely complemented her soft and pure complexion. At five-feet, six-inches tall, Françoise had developed into a stately woman with a magnificent body. Over the weeks that followed, Ahmad insisted on several occasions that Françoise join him for dinner following an all-day tour of Paris or a full day at the galleries. Following several excuses to refuse such invitations, she found herself running out of reasons to deny Ahmad's advances until she finally agreed to dinner at the Café Royal.

There were many memories for Françoise at the Café Royal and Monsieur Cardin was still there at the age of sixty-six. A widower with no children, the restaurant was his life. When Françoise and Ahmad arrived one evening for their first dinner together, Monsieur Cardin greeted Françoise with a warm smile and a huge embrace. Tears began to swell in his eyes. Françoise was like the daughter he never had, and the fondness he had for her father Louis extended easily to Françoise. He missed Louis as maitre d' following Louis's retirement a few years earlier, and seeing Françoise breathed new life into this tired old man. Ahmad was impressed with the attention and respect bestowed on Françoise by everyone at the Café Royal. The quiet table near the window overlooked the Seine and the cool May breezes were refreshing following a warm day of sunshine. The waiters were very attentive to the needs of the two special guests, being ever so careful not to appear overeager in their constant quest to assure that every aspect of the dinner was perfect. Ahmad was a connoisseur of wines and, as the wine steward recommended several fine choices, Ahmad asked specifically for a particular dry white wine, to which the steward immediately showed his approval.

Françoise literally hogged the conversation throughout their evening at the Café Royal, relating many stories of her tour leader days and before that as a youngster visiting her father who had worked for Monsieur Cardin for so many years. Glimpses of Dick came to mind on more than one occasion that night but Françoise shook these images from her mind as quickly as they came up. She had not returned to the Café Royal in over five years since Dick and she had been there. At first, it was a way of trying to wipe out this memory. Then, when she was expecting Dick's child, the embarrassment of people seeing her pregnant in the presence of her father or Monsieur Cardin would have crushed her father.

Over the next few weeks, Ahmad and Françoise dined often together and several times at the Café Royal. On all of these evenings, Ahmad was a perfect gentleman and host, completely fascinated by everything about Françoise. Unlike most of the women in Khatamori who had little opportunity or desire for independence, Françoise was very outspoken and did not hesitate to disagree with many of the prince's beliefs on religious matters and laws of state in his Middle Eastern country. This boldness was something Ahmad had never witnessed before from a woman. He wondered if there were women like this in Khatamori and, if so, how come he had never met one. Perhaps, he thought, he had never looked for this characteristic in the women he socialized with and that, if such women did exist, they dared not question a prince for fear of personal harm. He had never thought of himself as a powerful man although, as the son of a king, surely he was aware of the respect this commanded from his subjects.

As the month-long museum experience was coming to an end, Françoise was surprised by a question posed by Ahmad.

"With so many paintings by so many great artists, how does the museum protect itself from any harm or losses coming to the paintings? I see that you have many guards and barriers to the paintings, but how would you replace one of these great works if it was damaged or ruined?"

"They are irreplaceable, Ahmad, because they are originals. We can only ask an expert what they are worth, what someone would pay to own one of these, and then buy insurance to cover any loss we might have. There is no way we can replace it, but at least we can use the insurance money on the painting to buy others of equal value."

"Who does this? Who puts himself in a position to know what each of these is worth?" Ahmad questioned.

"Insurance companies hire art experts from all over the world to give their views on what such paintings will sell for and, after getting several different opinions, the insurance company offers to insure each painting or group of paintings by the same artist for a certain price each year. They, of course, place great demands on us to protect the paintings and to make sure that we keep them in perfect condition, or we can lose the insurance."

"Can you do this, Françoise—look at a painting and say what it is worth?"

"Oh, yes, Ahmad, but it takes time. You need to know the artist and his reputation and other paintings, and what those have sold for. You need to look at the quality of the painting, which might need repair because of its age, the type of paint used and whether there are any defects that are noticeable. But, yes, I have been one used by insurance companies to do this for paintings outside the Louvre. Why do you ask?"

"Now I know why my father sent me here to learn about all of this, Françoise." Ahmad stated with the look of someone who suddenly had found the Holy Grail. "My father has a very big collection of paintings from many artists from many countries. Some were gifts by rich oilmen from countries seeking to do business with us and some my father purchased from friends in exchange for money they needed for other purposes. He doesn't really know if he paid too dearly for these, he just paid whatever others said they were worth." Ahmad now began to laugh out loud, "Perhaps now he expects me to tell him what they are worth, it is all so amusing."

Françoise shared Ahmad's laughter as the end of their last day at the museum was nearing the end. He would be returning to Khatamori on a flight later that afternoon. As they strolled together through the galleries one last time, Ahmad held Françoise's hand with both of his own.

"May you be happy in your life, dear Françoise, for you have made me a wiser man in these days in Paris. It would be my honor if you would consider coming to Banra one day as my guest. We are a peaceful country and, although not as rich in history as your wonderful city, we have a tradition that is nearly a thousand years old. You would like Khatamori, I am certain of this. Until we meet again, my sweet flower, may Allah always bring you sunshine and good fortune." Ahmad kissed her hand in a very formal gesture, bowed courteously to her and turned to leave. As he headed out of sight in a far gallery exit, he never turned to look back to Françoise, and she stood there, still with her hand raised as if the kiss was still occurring on her hand.

As the prince disappeared from view, Françoise slowly headed back to her office. Her assistant met her at the door to her office and announced that a man had left a package for her. The man had insisted on personally putting the package on her desk to be sure that it was delivered properly.

On the desk was a small cylinder, carefully wrapped in silk and tied together at the top with thin leather string. Under the package was an envelope addressed to her and sealed in a red wax symbol. She opened the envelope and read the note, "Think of me from time to time, Ahmad."

Françoise opened the silk covering and there she gazed upon a miniature urn of pure gold with a matching cover to the urn. As she lifted the cover, her eyes gently closed as she absorbed the scent of the *Flower of Heaven.* Under the urn were several sticks of the incense as well. Françoise would treasure this gift.

CHAPTER 12

Claude was pleased with the attention that Françoise had given to Prince Ahmad and with the compensation the museum had received from him for the tutorial over the last month. Françoise was also rewarded with a week's vacation and an increase in her already high compensation. Her mother and father were not aware of how much Françoise earned, but it was more in one year than her father had earned in the last five years he had worked at the restaurant. It was no wonder that she was always buying them items for the house that she knew they wanted but could never afford. She would also leave money with her mother for household expenses, making sure that Louis would not know because it would have embarrassed him to find out. Françoise would drive to their home in her new car, a Peugeot, and would take her parents all over France on sightseeing excursions and to allow them to spend more time together. These moments were precious to her, for she knew that her parents would soon not be able to travel much longer given their ages and fragile health.

Following a week away from the museum, Françoise was happy to return to her role at the Louvre. The remainder of July and August were high tourist season in Paris, which meant extra gallery tours and more money for the museum. When September arrived, Françoise was again exhausted but anticipated a much lighter traffic in the gallery in the coming months.

"Bonjour, Françoise," Claude echoed as he strode into her office one afternoon in September. "You look like you could use another vacation, or at least some time away from the museum. I have just the thing for you," as he was holding a letter of some sort and handed it to Françoise.

Monsieur Claude Gagnon
Directeur Generale
The Louvre
Paris, France
Dear Monsieur Gagnon,

It is with deep sincerity that I extend my gratitude to you for your excellent learning experience to my son, Ahmad, the crown prince of Khatamori, during his stay in Paris in May of this year. It has always been my wish that Ahmad learn more about famous places in the world so that, someday, he may pass on this knowledge to his own children once he succeeds me as ruler of our beloved kingdom.

The palace in Banra has accumulated many pieces of art as gifts from other countries over many years. I am not qualified to know the value of such art, and Ahmad, although now more understanding of such value, does not pretend to know it either. Since the palace has over forty rooms of such art treasure, it would be wise for me to know how important it is to protect each painting. Ahmad has told me that a member of your staff, Mademoiselle Françoise Dupont, does this rating of paintings and can determine their value. Such information would be important to me. I would like to invite you and Mademoiselle Dupont to Banra for this purpose at whatever cost you feel is justified to fulfill the task.

The climate in Khatamori in October and November is quite pleasant and warm, and you would be my guests for as long as the review is needed. My son and I await your reply.

Royal Highness of Khatamori
King Fatam

This is more than a coincidence, Françoise told herself. Ahmad had clearly convinced his father that getting an expert to evaluate his art collection would be a smart thing to do, never leading on that this was also a way for him to get Françoise to his native land. Regardless of the motive, Françoise was intrigued by the letter and quickly agreed to go to Khatamori in early November, a time in Paris when the weather begins to get colder and the frequency of daily tours lessens significantly to a few school tours. She would not be leaving the gallery during an overly busy period and would welcome the warmer climate, not to mention the thought of seeing Ahmad again.

Claude, on the other hand, announced that October and November were not good months for him to be away from the Louvre since he would be meeting frequently during this period with the governing board to discuss plans for future expansion and to also discuss the results of the recent tourist season. As the board members came from all over France to attend these meetings, it would not be appropriate to attempt to reschedule the meeting dates at such a late date in September. Françoise would have to go without him.

* * *

Françoise arrived in Banra to eighty-degree sunshine and was immediately greeted by Ahmad himself along with an entourage of servants. Ahmad was dressed very formally in a long robe with full turban and jewelry on practically every finger. Françoise recalled Ahmad's insistence that while in public, a crown prince must always be formally presented before the multitudes. A large crowd of Khatamorans were on hand to catch a glimpse of who would merit the prince himself to appear to greet a visitor. Surely a head of state or another Arab chieftain of sorts. It was no wonder that the chatter among the curious onlookers somewhat startled Françoise as she approached Ahmad.

The sight of a Westerner dressed in non-Arab clothing, and a woman as well, with no head or facial covering, addressing a crown prince brought gasps of disbelief from many. Françoise had not been prepared for such a disruptive greeting and, to Ahmad, it showed. In a very warm display of greeting to Françoise, Ahmad's chief servant, the same one who had accompanied him to Paris, provided Françoise with a veil and cloak covering as she approached the smiling prince.

"My dearest Françoise, the *Flower of Heaven* be with you again as I welcome you to Khatamori. Come, let us depart for my home, my servants will see to your belongings," Ahmad announced as he literally bowed to greet Françoise. Again, this brought a sigh to the crowd who had never witnessed such behavior from a leader in their country. Ahmad paid little attention to their noise and extended both hands to Françoise in a welcoming manner. Françoise blushed, an uncontrollable blush, as she too was now overwhelmed by the splendor and majesty of the man who, in Paris, did not want to stand out in public. His very presence at the Banra airport and the reaction it brought to the populace immediately struck Françoise at the magnitude of respect and power that Ahmad held among his own people.

As Françoise began following Ahmad, he introduced her to a young captain in the Khatamori Guard, Captain Answa Talon, a boyhood friend of the prince and nephew to King Fatam. Talon greeted Françoise with a stern handshake and immediately led the entourage toward the limousine waiting at the entrance to the small terminal. Ahmad pointed out to Françoise that the royal palace was about ten miles south of the airport and that this would allow her an opportunity to see some of the country along the route. Ahmad was easily comfortable at highlighting various mosques and marketplaces along the way. Françoise could not help but notice that no one appeared destitute and the sights were quite beautiful, even if mostly barren. It was also evident that the limousine was recognizable by all in whose path it traveled as citizens bowed out of respect for royalty passing by.

Although a small country, the discovery of oil years earlier had a real boom to the economy of the country and to the riches of the royal family. Ahmad was an only child, his mother the queen having died years earlier during the birth of his younger brother who also died a mere three days after his birth. King Fatam was in his early fifties and, while many Arabs had many wives and children, Fatam still mourned the death of his one and only love. He could never get into any kind of relationship which, in his mind, would allow him to forget about his years with the queen. And so, Ahmad was the focus of the king's attention and accompanied him almost everywhere throughout his youth and early adulthood. It was as if he too was celibate without even realizing it. It is difficult to become a womanizer, even when you're in the royal family, if there are few women presented before you that interest you. Fatam was not one to live a lavish life even though he was worth hundreds of millions of dollars. His courtesy, however, always welcomed other dignitaries from surrounding allied countries, which is mostly how he had amassed his vast collection of art over the years. Once these dignitaries realized that Fatam appreciated good art, it automatically led to their bestowing more gifts whenever they visited. Fatam, in return, would visit the other Middle Eastern countries on rare occasions, but was quite content in attending to the affairs of state within Khatamori.

While Ahmad was the only heir apparent to the throne and was involved in dealings with other oil-generating Arab countries, Fatam focused on the orderly running of the country, including the areas of defense and security with the son of his late brother. Should anything happen to Fatam and Ahmad was incapable of serving and had no sons of his own, Answa would be next in line to assume the throne as the closest living relative. While Ahmad and Answa had been friends since childhood, Answa was envious of Ahmad's role in comparison to his own more miniscule status in the royal family. Answa had three wives and eight children and frowned on the lack of succession on the Fatam and Ahmad side of the crown. He had more than once chastised Ahmad at having no wives, almost to the point of accusing him of not fulfilling the wishes of Allah by remaining unmarried. Ahmad, on the other hand, would insist to Answa that he would wed when, and only when, he found someone worthy of being a princess and someone he truly loved, not before.

The limousine turned off the main road onto the entrance of a long and gated driveway surrounded by armed guards at the gate. A ten-foot wall covered the outer perimeter of the grounds for nearly as far as you could see. Françoise was amazed at the beautifully manicured entryway aligned with plush green foliage intermingled among the palm trees. The thousand-foot drive led to a gigantic stairway entrance to the palace, a sweeping modern five-story complex nearly as immense as the Louvre itself.

"Come, Françoise, let me show you the wing you will be staying in. That will give you some time to rest from your journey. The servants will see to your belongings. Later today, I will give you a tour of the palace and then we will meet with my father for dinner this evening. Now it will be I who conducts the tour and not you," he smiled as he escorted her down a large marble-floored hallway.

Françoise could not help but notice the many paintings hanging on the walls along this hallway. She recognized many immediately but she hesitated to comment on these while the grandeur of the place overwhelmed her. Following what seemed like a ten-minute walk, Ahmad stopped in front of huge mahogany doors and pushed them open.

"Voila, Françoise, I hope you find the rooms to your liking. I will have one of the servants come for you in a few hours. Until then, may you rest."

The white shiny marble floor and white stucco walls leading to a canopied and veiled bed with satin sheets were overshadowed by the bright sunlight emanating from the open doors leading to a terrace overlooking the beautiful grounds to the rear of the palace. An adjoining large bathroom displayed a freestanding bathtub and to the side shelves with various sized towels, soaps, and lotions. Not to her surprise but to her delight, Françoise detected the fragrance that she had been introduced to by Ahmad in Paris. To the left of the balcony doors was a sofa and cushioned chair separated by a floor lamp and positioned perfectly to observe the city below. Incense burned in several small containers positioned in different corners of the room and the aroma of the *Flower of Heaven* permeated throughout. As she headed for a better view on the terrace, she was interrupted by a knock on the door and servants delivering her luggage. One of the servants pointed to a set of double louver doors and, as he swung them open, merely pointed inside at the vast wardrobe that had been placed hanging in a closet.

"A woman servant will be here at five to assist you to prepare for dinner with his highness, the king, and the crown prince."

Touché, thought Françoise. She was now in Ahmad's country and would be expected to respect the customs and proper dress before the king, just as Ahmad had done by dressing like a Parisian in Paris. Perhaps it would not be so bad, she thought.

A few hours later, a knock at the door awakened Françoise as she rested peacefully in her robe, a beautiful silk wrap that had been strewn across the bed when she first arrived. As she opened her bedroom door, there stood two smiling women servants hardly able to understand a word Françoise spoke, but very qualified to assist her in the proper manner of dress to select for the evening, from veil to Arabian-style shoes, to jewelry and oils. As she gazed at herself in the floor-length mirror some time later, the servants waited for a look of approval from Françoise at the result. She smiled and as she nodded her approval, she blushed uncontrollably as she looked at herself again as if in disbelief that she was about to embark on a new venture in a strange new world.

At six, another knock at the door led one of the two servants to respond and there, in all his majesty and splendor, stood Ahmad, in full-length robe complete with an elegant Arab headdress, jewelry around his neck and on most fingers. He froze momentarily as he caught a glimpse of Françoise. She was stunning and like no one he had ever seen in his own country. He smiled broadly and she returned the smile with one of her own.

"Françoise, you are breathless, so very beautiful in your evening wear, my father will be pleased. Before we go, however, let me show you how to cover your face for now until my father instructs you to remove it. Otherwise, it would be difficult to eat that way, wouldn't it?" he joked as he approached her.

She laughed out loud at this show of humor, something she had not as yet seen in Ahmad. He was pleased that she found this amusing and proceeded to have one of the servants affix the facial veil properly. He then held out his hand for her to accompany him as they left her room.

Françoise turned cordially to the servants and merely gestured, "Merci."

As Ahmad led her from room to room toward the royal family's private quarters and the dining areas for visitors, she kept glancing constantly at the immensely high ceilings and the paintings and ornaments hanging everywhere she turned. So much money and power, she thought, from such a gentle person. Hopefully, the king would be no different. They approached an entryway with servants on each side leading to a torch-lit room alive with servants everywhere, bustling about with a selection of dishes being brought to a spacious and gleaming wooden table that certainly could accommodate a dozen people or more. Seated at the far end of the table was Fatam with Answa and one of his wives to his left.

Ahmad approached his father. "Father, allow me to introduce Mademoiselle Françoise Dupont from the Louvre in Paris."

Fatam replied ever so cleverly, "Why yes, my son, I know that the Louvre is in Paris. Welcome to my country and to my home, my dear Mademoiselle Dupont. I am looking forward to your assistance this week in finding out if these gifts I have been receiving for years have been worth hanging, or should I be thinking about hanging instead the ones who gave them to me." His smile as he spoke immediately put Françoise at ease as he held her extended hand in both of his as a gesture of sincerity.

"Please call me Françoise, Your Highness, everyone does."

"Only if you call me Fatam. You see, I am really not, Your Highness, am I? Old time customs and formalities sometimes are just that, old time. I am fortunate to be the son of the former king, it is not something I asked for, but if I must continue the line of rulers that goes back hundreds of years, so be it. Please, you may remove your veil. My son speaks highly of you, but he did not mention to me how beautiful you were. Beauty and intelligence. That is quite a combination I would say. You remind me of …," the thought drifted away from Fatam as he asked Françoise to sit on the right by his side with Ahmad next to her.

Françoise did not remember what food was served that night, as she was more engrossed in the warmth of the conversation between her and Fatam, all to the satisfaction of Ahmad who watched calmly at how Françoise handled herself with his father.

Answa hardly spoke and appeared more puzzled at the attention given to a foreign woman. The wife at his side never spoke, which Françoise found strange. Perhaps women in Khatamori spoke only when spoken to or when given permission to do so, a custom not familiar to a French woman.

Later that evening, as Ahmad took Françoise for a stroll in the beautiful gardens within the palace grounds, she asked him about the silence and almost nonexistence of Answa's wife at dinner.

"You must understand, Françoise, that many wives are allowed in our country and each has a purpose. This wife, Sakara, almost always attends the dinners and receptions at the palace. She hardly speaks and Answa likes it that way since she will never embarrass him in front of guests by what she says. Answa has no children from Sakara; his eight children are from Fari and Nalia. While it may seem strange to you, to Answa and many others in Khatamori, it is how it is done. My father, I suppose, is an exception. He has married but once, to my mother and, when she died five years ago, he could not see himself even looking for someone to replace her with."

"And what of you, Ahmad, where is your wife, or should I say wives?" Françoise asked so innocently.

"I must be like my father more than I thought, because I have not wed as of this day, something that troubles my father greatly. Each generation of our family seems to be different than the last and I will marry the one who will be by my side and raise my children for as long as we both shall live."

As they continued to walk toward the section of the grounds leading back to her room, they were both now quiet as they occasionally glanced at each other along the way. That night, Françoise slept very well.

The next several days encompassed a mixture of serious evaluating of the massive list of art throughout the palace and seeing as much of the sights of this tiny country as she could see with Ahmad as her guide. They visited the oil fields and refinery, the ancient burial grounds of his ancestors and even took time to visit small shops in the marketplace in Banra. The outer limits of Banra were primarily made up of small villages with simple dwellings of stone, but no areas looked ragged or downtrodden.

Each night, however, following dinner in the palace, sometimes with Fatam and on one night with Ahmad alone, they would return to the gardens where thousands of stars seemed to light up the night and provide them with perfect scenery. They were getting to know a great deal about each other and their relationship began to become more serious.

"What would you do, Françoise, if you were living here all the time and no longer had the Louvre in Paris to go to? How would you change things or what would make you happy in a place such as this?"

"I don't know, Ahmad, I guess knowing that I could do something to make the women more respected and not just objects to be used as Answa does. I could never be happy without a way to speak about things that are important to me, and I don't believe that women here seem to get much of a chance to do anything of importance in the country. Most do not appear to be encouraged to become educated, to become doctors, teachers, or heads of state. Where are they, Ahmad, who would I talk to if few are allowed to speak at all? Your father seems ready to accept changes; he has already broken some old customs by not remarrying or having several wives, hasn't he? I see changes all the time at the Louvre, Ahmad, and so it must be in Khatamori as well if your country is to become truly rich in more than just oil. You are not the only one who needs to learn about what else goes on in the world. Others must be allowed to do the same."

"To break this way of life is not an easy thing, Françoise, it has been this way for as long as I can remember and for as long as my father can remember. We are a peaceful country and very protective of our ways. Perhaps it is time to try a new way, perhaps."

CHAPTER 13

"Father, Françoise will be leaving at the end of the week and there is something I need to discuss with you," Ahmad said to Fatam after he returned from his daily early morning walk on the grounds of the palace. Fatam enjoyed the quiet and serenity at this time of day and often would reflect on his late wife and the years they had spent together raising Ahmad.

"What is it, my son?" Fatam asked as he put his arm around Ahmad's shoulders.

The silence that followed only raised Fatam's curiosity even more. "Tell me, Ahmad, something seems to be troubling you, I can sense it,"

"When you and my mother first met, did you know then that she would be the one?"

"That was so long ago, my son, but, no, I did not even think that we would end together. As you know, your mother was strong and no one was going to tell her how to do things and she was too outspoken for a woman in Khatamori where women's voices are seldom heard or listened to. I think that is what first struck me about her; she was not to be just one of many wives to someone. Why do you ask, or do I sense the departing of Françoise more than just news you want to share with me?"

"I once told you, father, that I would marry and give you a grandson before you left this place to be reunited with my mother, but that, like you, I would marry for love. I see Answa with his three wives and very little respect for any of them and I do not want this for my life. I say this, father, because I think Françoise may be the one but she is like my mother, wanting women to be treated with more dignity and respect then they have now. She would not be happy with just being a queen someday; she needs and wants very much to be more. Perhaps she is not aware of what she could do or be for the people here. I know she enjoys everything we have here, but I am not so certain she is ready to give up what she has for what she knows very little of."

"Only Françoise can answer those questions, my son, and only when you are certain that it is time to hear her answers, even if the answers are not what you would like them to be," replied Fatam. "A marriage is not to be taken lightly and, although your cousin shows little respect for his wives, they accept their roles and do not do or say anything that would make Answa angry. Your mother, on the other hand, was very different and we often had disagreements on her attempts to bring Khatamori women to higher levels of recognition. If she were alive today, I believe she would have succeeded. One of the biggest changes she made was in getting women more educated by starting their education earlier and encouraging them to seek positions in medicine, finance, and teaching instead of merely being used by their husbands to raise children. After she died, there was no one to continue what she had started, and we are back to our old ways with our women," Fatam went on.

As Ahmad and his father strolled together in the gardens below, Françoise stood in her robe on the terrace of her bedroom and watched them. Such a relationship between father and son meant a great deal to her and she remembered her early childhood and the many strolls throughout Paris she had had with her own father years ago. Her mother and father were both retired now and leading a quiet life, totally unaware of the life Françoise had built for herself from her days as a bus tour guide. Her travels to this Middle Eastern country were already more than her parents had ever done and she was still only in her twenties.

Later that morning, she saw Ahmad by himself in the gardens and he appeared to be deep in thought. As she approached him, he turned to greet her with a vibrant smile and both hands extended to meet hers.

"I trust you slept well, Françoise," he said. "I come here often; it is to me a very beautiful and quiet place for me to think about things. Things I would like to do, things I would like to say and wonder what will become of me today, tomorrow, and who knows when."

"And what great words of wisdom have you come up with this day, Ahmad?" Françoise echoed smilingly.

"I believe I have a dilemma, Françoise, and I do not know how to deal with it," he replied as he gazed toward the sun away from her. "There is a woman out there, a very lovely woman, who intrigues me to no end. She is intelligent, ambitious, and not aware of the different customs that exist outside her own country. She would fight to change some of these customs if she was given the chance to do so, perhaps too quickly, which would upset some people who want to keep the old ways. Because I have seen other ways in my travels, I have seen how change can sometimes be a good thing, and I believe that, in time, changes in our customs would be well-received, even if such changes were led by a woman, something that my mother began years ago but, that faded away as quickly as my memory of her has over the years."

"This woman," Françoise asked, "does she feel the same about you, that you are also intriguing, kind, intelligent, and very attracted to her, even though she needs to and would very much like to learn more about the ways of your people?"

"I don't, know, Françoise," Ahmad replied as he turned to face her, the morning sun radiating on her soft complexion. "I have grown very fond of her since we met some months ago and I have even brought her here once to see what Khatamori is like. She seemed to adapt very quickly and appeared to even enjoy the way women dress here."

Ahmad now gazed at Françoise in a serious manner and continued, "I would need to know if she would like this to go further or if she wants to remain at home and not pursue this any longer."

"And where is home to this woman you speak of, Ahmad?" Françoise queried in innocence.

"Home is now Paris, Françoise, but home tomorrow could be Khatamori," Ahmad softly replied as he approached her tenderly.

Françoise's face blushed so much that she began to hold her cheeks with both hands. She turned away from Ahmad so that he would not notice and her heart began to beat so fast that she began to lose her breath as she tried to compose herself.

She turned and they locked in an embrace that seemed to last forever as she gushed, "Do you know what you are asking, Ahmad, I cannot believe how foolish of me not to see this coming. I am overwhelmed and do not know what to say."

"No words need be spoken for now, Françoise; I only know that we could be so much more to each other in time. I need only to know that one day we could have a life together here in Khatamori if there is a chance that you have feelings for me as I do so very much for you."

Françoise put her arms around Ahmad and kissed him very passionately, her entire body now alive with emotion as she held nothing back. "Oh, Ahmad, I have had feelings for you since you wore the French clothing in Paris, since you would open doors to restaurants for me and pull out my chair at our table. When you left Paris, I was very sad to see you go, and when the letter came to the Louvre for me to come to Khatamori, my heart began to beat again. I do like your country very much and I do have strong feelings about your way of life, but I also believe in you and your father and your willingness to allow for change here. There is so much I need to know and learn about your people and how they would welcome a stranger, a foreigner, to be with you."

"And what of the Louvre and your very successful career?" Ahmad asked as he continued the conversation, still clinging to Françoise, not wanting to let go.

"I must go back to Paris and see if my heart can free itself from there to be here instead. And now that I have seen Khatamori at a glance, perhaps in the remaining days before I go, you can show me so much more of the customs of your people. I would very much like to learn as much as I can until then."

The remaining days that week were a whirlwind of activities: travelling throughout the country, visiting schools and businesses, and talking to as many locals as Françoise could. But the Friday arrived when she was scheduled to leave and her return flight had been booked weeks before. At the airport outside of Banra, Ahmad was terribly saddened by her departure and addressed her one last time before she boarded her plane.

"Françoise, these last few weeks have been more than I ever imagined and I realize now that you are the one who was chosen to be with me. My father sends his deepest wishes to you for a safe journey back to Paris and also will pray that you arrive at your difficult decision that would take you on an everlasting journey far beyond today. He has also grown quite fond of you and I have told him of my love for you, a love that I do not give so easily. You are the judge of your own destiny; I will be here awaiting your decision."

"I have so much to attend to, Ahmad, so many duties that Claude relies on me to handle. I don't know when or how I can end my life at the Louvre, or even if it is to happen at all. I need time to do all of this and I don't know how long it will take for me to decide," she stated as she held him with both hands.

Ahmad, as the royal prince, was not allowed to hug and kiss her in public though he found it very difficult to hold back as many observers realized whose presence they were in.

"Today is the twentieth of November and, in six months' time, the twentieth of May of next year, I will be here at this very spot to greet you. I pray that you are here as well on that day. Until then, I will count the days that we are apart," Ahmad proclaimed.

With that farewell, Françoise boarded the plane back to Paris.

CHAPTER 14

May 20, 1957, seemed so far away that, in the following weeks and months since her return to the Louvre on November 20, Françoise was once again bombarded with various demands in her work.

Claude was enthusiastically pleased with the service she had provided King Fatam and showed her a letter of praise from the king that he had recently received. Following a board of trustees meeting at the Louvre in early December, Claude announced to Françoise that she had been promoted to Deputy Director of the Louvre. This announcement was splattered on the business pages of every French newspaper along with a photo of Françoise being congratulated by Claude.

Word of Françoise's promotion reached Ahmad in Khatamori and he realized that her decision now would be even more difficult to make.

On her desk at the Louvre, Françoise had circled the date of May 20 on her calendar as 1957 began but seemed to evolve at a snail's pace. This was a slow season at the galleries, after the Christmas holidays and before school breaks when many students visited the museum. It was a perfect time, however, for Françoise to begin delegating more of her duties to several other supervisors. As she did so, Claude began to notice that her attention to her new role did not meet his expectations and he confronted her to inquire about what seemed to be troubling her.

"Claude, my time in Khatamori turned out to be much more than evaluating King Fatam's art collection. Ahmad and I became very attracted to each other, something I never expected. I think of him every day, Claude, and he has asked me to become his future queen in Khatamori."

"This is a very huge decision, Françoise, one that seldom ever arises to anyone, especially someone from outside the country. Your future here is quite good; the trustees believe that someday you would replace me as Director. You've worked hard to reach this level and leaving this behind is something I can't imagine you doing," Claude said as he clearly expressed his disbelief at what he was hearing. "When you have thought this through, and you realize what you are thinking of doing, I am certain you will decide to stay at the Louvre."

Françoise would inform Claude of her decision once she came to it but, in the meantime, she did everything she could to remain immersed in her daily routine. Anything that would delay her from confronting the issue.

Over the following months leading into March, Françoise had not heard at all from Ahmad, as he had told her he would do to give her time to arrive at a decision and to begin transitioning her work to others. Perhaps not intentional, but Françoise had already begun to delegate tour arrangements, budget preparations, gallery special events, and other duties that she normally would personally handle.

So it was on a chilly morning in April, when she was in her office arranging items on her desk that she gazed upon the box in the corner of the bookshelf nearby. She opened it very carefully and the aroma from the incense inside totally mesmerized her as she closed her eyes. Her thoughts were now in Khatamori and all she could imagine was being in Ahmad's arms again.

Claude did not take the news well, but understood that Françoise had made her decision after much thought. She informed him that she would be leaving her position on May 5 in order to give her time to settle her affairs at home, announce her plans to her parents, and make flight arrangements: this time a one-way ticket.

Before she left Claude's office, however, she turned to him and began, "You have been my mentor, my friend, my savior for all these years and I have tried to be a good student, a daughter you never had and someone you could always rely on. I ask but one thing of you, would you come to my wedding when the day arrives?" They hugged each other for several minutes, both very much in tears.

"Your Highness, I would be honored to be there," he finally replied.

* * *

On May 20, there was only one flight that went to Banra and it departed at 7:00 a.m. that morning. Françoise was extremely nervous as she boarded the plane for the five-hour flight. Had she made a foolish decision, would Ahmad really be at the airport in Banra to greet her, or would she be totally devastated if no one appeared there? She suddenly had an urge to get off the plane when the roar of the engines began and the plane started to taxi toward the runway. This seemed to calm her down as she sat back in her seat. Her decision had been made and in her heart she knew that Ahmad would be there.

When the plane finally arrived several hours later, she headed down the staircase toward the small terminal. Before she passed through the outside glass doors, two attendants stood at attention and both doors were opened by them as she entered the terminal. A crowd of people immediately could be seen gazing at her as they suddenly cleared an opening for her to reveal Ahmad standing there in his most regal attire and a smile that made her realize that this truly was the man of her dreams.

As she approached, he extended both hands toward Françoise and, in a manner hardly seen by the local Khatamorans, he kissed her and held her in his arms for quite some time. The buzz in the crowd and the warmth shown by Ahmad caused the people to break out in a loud applause and cheer; their prince had finally found his mate.

While still in an embrace, Ahmad whispered in Françoise's ear, "Welcome home, my princess, welcome to the flower of heaven."

In June and July of that year, Françoise began to seriously get involved in the country and began assembling an agenda of items that she believed would become topics of discussion with Ahmad and his father after their wedding, areas that mainly concerned the rights and opportunities, or lack thereof, for the women of Khatamori. She visited schools, hospitals, mosques, and many business establishments in several cities outside Banra and quickly became recognized as the Madame Princess by many at first who were cautious in dealing with her but, eventually, Princess Farah gained respect that often eluded women in the kingdom. The name Farah was chosen because it meant "joy and happiness" in Arabic and that is what she wanted to convey to the people. Fatam was very pleased with Princess Farah and could see many of the same feisty qualities in her that he had seen in Ahmad's mother. It was like the spirit of his wife had been reawakened.

Over the next several years, although Fatam's wishes for a successor to Ahmad had not occurred, Farah continued to please both Ahmad and his father in her role as the crusader for women. Khatamoran men, however, were not so enthused at losing control of their virtual women in bondage. Answa, in particular, found that all three of his wives constantly spoke the praises of Farah for the new things they were now allowed to do like driving a car, not covering their faces with a veil all the time in public, attending school, and even serving as spokespersons for businesses throughout the kingdom. Farah had assembled a team of advisors who continually sought to introduce new ventures for women. All the women adored her. Answa, on the other hand, wondered why a woman, a foreigner so concerned about the rights of women beyond their duties as mothers and loyal servants to their husbands, had no children of her own after years of marriage to Ahmad. His curiosity would lead him to Paris eventually, the place where the relationship first began. This investigation would uncover Farah's past in due time.

In 1986, nearly thirty years later, King Fatam passed away in his sleep at the age of eighty-five. It was not unexpected but, nevertheless, Khatamorans mourned the death of their beloved leader for weeks until the coronation of Ahmad as the new ruler to succeed his father. Ahmad, in recent years, had not been well as he suffered from kidney problems, a reason most people attributed to his inability to procreate a direct heir in the family. Farah's physical health did not indicate a problem in her ability to bear children. Answa now, however, knew differently.

CHAPTER 15

Carl and Judy Elliott had been married for nearly five years by 1952. Carl worked for a large glass manufacturer in Elmira, New York, after accepting an engineering position with the company right out of college from the University of Rhode Island in 1947.

Carl's career had a lot of promise as he was perceived by management as a hard worker ready to take on any assignment thrown his way. He first was assigned to a supervisory position on the second shift at the plant and his efficiency and production results soon caught the attention of his plant manager, Tony Almeida. Carl was soon transferred to the main day shift where the plant ran more at full capacity than the evening shift. After a few years, Carl's continued performance led to his promotion to Assistant Plant Manager. The only thing that seemed to be missing in Carl and Judy's life was the fact that they had not been blessed with any children. Following recent tests to determine if anything was genetically wrong with their ability to have children, the Elliotts were told that nothing was wrong and that, at times, couples can go for years trying to conceive, but with no success. Carl's wife, Judy, suffered from mild depression each time the conversation at dinner parties turned to children and most of their guests bragged about their own.

Perhaps believing that a change of scenery might help her, Judy welcomed the news from Carl that he had accepted an assignment to assist the company in opening a glass plant in Paris, France. Carl would likely spend one year getting the operation up and running at which time he would be reassigned to a new position back in the States. Carl saw this as a huge opportunity and one where the rewards could enable him to move up the corporate ladder faster than he even anticipated.

In May of that year, the Elliotts arrived in the City of Lights and moved into spacious accommodations in a six-room, two-story apartment on rue du Temple, just a short walk to the Hotel de Ville. Carl's company had provided for these living quarters at no charge and the money the Elliotts saved by not having to pay rent would go a long way to increasing their finances. The extra money would allow Carl and Judy to purchase a home when they returned to New York in the summer of 1953.

May is lovely in Paris as blossoms begin to appear and sunny warmer days become more common as each day passes. As part of the company policy, all employees and spouses who were assigned to a foreign location were asked to take a complete physical examination with the local company doctor shortly after arriving to that country. It was no different for the company's location in Paris and on this spring day, the Elliotts headed to the company doctor's office for the routine exam. The office of Dr. Jean-Louis Matthieu, a general practitioner in Paris, was located a short walk from the Elliotts' apartment. Dr. Matthieu had a regular local practice but had also obtained the contract for the company physicals after having met a company official at a social gathering in the early stages of planning for the upcoming plant opening.

"Have either of you any particular conditions or ailments that you would like to tell me about?" exclaimed Dr. Matthieu, "as I find all your physical conditions to be in order."

Carl and Judy looked quizzically at each other and hesitated for a moment before Judy blurted, "We seem to be having difficulty in having a child and our doctor in the US found no reason for this."

Dr. Matthieu concurred that these things happen among couples often only to one day discover that the wife has finally become pregnant, perhaps even many years later when all hope had been lost at ever conceiving.

"Of course," Dr. Matthieu mentioned, "you could always adopt a child if all else fails and you really want children. Even if you eventually become pregnant, the worse that it would be is that you'd have another child instead of just one. Adopting is quite easy in Paris these days and the orphanages are filled with children, even babies, hoping to become part of some loving family. Why just the other day, I delivered twins to a young mother who was unmarried and could not provide for the babies, so she planned to give them up for adoption at the Orphanage of the Sisters of Mercy in Giverny. There are children there all the way up to twelve years old who have never been adopted. Et bien, something to consider."

Carl knew that Judy believed she was less of a woman because of this and sex in the household was rare. Instead, Carl delved into his work at the plant and often arrived home late for dinner in the evening. This would upset Judy all the more since the one exciting moment of her day was preparing a large dinner for the two of them on most nights. Fridays and Saturdays were usually spent at some local restaurants with other American couples also temporarily assigned to Paris.

On this particular day in early August, Carl cheerily entered the apartment with a bouquet of fresh flowers from a street vendor and smiled broadly as he kissed his wife on both cheeks, a French custom he rather liked.

Judy was somewhat startled and blurted out, "And to what do I owe these lovely flowers to, Mr. Elliott? Did you get a raise or did you get news that we're being transferred back to Elmira sooner than you thought?"

Carl shrugged at the sarcasm as quickly as it came from Judy's lips. "Judy, my love, we were talking at lunch today, a bunch of us and some local guys, and Henri Latour showed me pictures of his two kids, two gorgeous little girls, ages five and seven. It seems that they didn't have children of their own until just a few years ago. His wife had been part of the French underground during the war, had been shot, but somehow survived. Since then, they couldn't have children and decided to adopt the two girls from that same orphanage that Dr. Matthieu mentioned. Henri tells me that since the war, the orphanage has more children than it can handle and welcomes good couples who are interested in adopting children. They have children of all young ages, even babies and, I was wondering if, maybe, we could just visit there and…", his voice trailed off as quietly as the sound of a distant train.

"Oh, Carl, what are you saying, how are they going to allow Americans to even think about adopting a local child. There must be rules against this over here," Judy shot back. "You and I raising a family would be wonderful and I would love nothing better having my own."

"So would I, Judy, my love, so would I. Henri tells me that it's been done before, through the blessing of the American Embassy and the French government. The nuns go by the rules and Henri can set us up to visit the place next week if we want. C'mon, sweetie, let's do something to light that spark in our marriage again.

The following day, Carl asked Henri to call the orphanage to see if it was possible for them to visit on Saturday or Sunday. As Henri made the telephone call, you could sense the anxiety on Carl's face as he awaited Henri's response following what seemed like thirty minutes on the phone with one of the nuns from the orphanage. There would be many questions to answer and someone had to accompany the Elliotts to the orphanage since they did not speak enough fluent French to get by yet. Henri volunteered to help out.

That August, the Elliotts adopted an infant from the orphanage and named him Robert Conrad Elliott, deciding not to change the first name that had been given to the child by the natural mother. Judy's eyes beamed as she held her new baby and Carl could immediately see the wonderful effect that this had on the couple. The Elliotts were now a family and no one in the US would even know that their child was adopted, not that it mattered. Robert was truly now part of the Elliott family.

Over the next several months, Carl noticed how happy Judy was tending to her new baby. Carl could notice himself breaking away from work on occasion just to rush home and spend time with their new addition. The new bonding made the months fly by and Carl was amazed at how quickly his stay in France had passed. This calmness and elated behavior from Judy enabled Carl to focus more clearly on setting up the operations of the new glass plant much sooner than even he anticipated. As a result of completing his assignment by March, 1953, rather than June of that year, Carl's company rewarded the Elliotts with a return passage to the United States on the Queen Mary luxury liner, a beautiful ending to a wonderful year.

Upon his return to Elmira, Carl was immediately assigned to head the company's specialty glass operations in Louisville, Kentucky, a much larger facility than the Elmira plant. The glass manufactured in Louisville was for fireplace inserts, sliding glass doors, windshields, and other specific usages and involved a diverse sales force and many different markets. Carl was pleased and the three of them headed for Kentucky within the next month.

Over the following ten years, the Elliotts raised Robert and his younger brother Ben. Ironically, Judy became pregnant just two years after adopting Robert. Bob Elliott was a natural athlete, joining the local little league at age eight and getting better and better as each season passed. By the time he was fifteen, Bob had grown to nearly six feet tall and was quite muscular. As he prepared to enter high school after graduating from St. Mary's Junior High, Bob was not only a top baseball player, but his height naturally took him to playing basketball as well. Louisville South was a huge high school and Bob's warm and loving personality and talent enabled him to excel in both sports and academics. After graduating as the class valedictorian in 1970, he headed for Louisville University on a full scholarship, agreeing to play both basketball and baseball there. It was during his freshman year at Louisville that Bob met Julie Laflamme, a pre-med major from Somerville, Massachusetts. Julie's tough academic schedule did not allow her to attend many sporting events but it was just what Bob needed, someone who liked him for the person he was rather than because he was a varsity athlete. They fell madly in love and tried deeply not to let their passion for each other interfere with each of their professional plans as graduation approached in 1974.

Julie was destined for medical school at Vanderbilt University in Nashville and Bob was mulling an offer to sign with the Boston Red Sox organization. As an outstanding outfielder for Louisville, Bob had achieved a .380 batting average in his senior year, blasting twenty-one home runs. He also was known for his remarkably strong and accurate arm as an outfielder, all the qualities of a potential major leaguer. Julie, on the other hand, sincerely thought that she would have little time for any relationship while attending Vanderbilt where the demands of her time in medical school would not allow much of a social life. So, Bob and Julie reluctantly agreed to put their personal plans on hold as they both needed to focus on their professional needs. They agreed, however, to write to each other and to plan to meet somewhere over the Christmas holidays each year, plans that would somehow never materialize.

Bob had a successful rookie season for the Red Sox in 1975, spending half of the season on the AA affiliate of the team but being promoted in July of that year to the Sox' AAA team in the Pacific Coast League. During the off-season, and especially during the winter holidays, Bob returned home to Louisville. Each time he attempted to arrange to meet Julie during this period, each time he would get a reply by mail from her stating she would only have a few days off in December and felt it necessary to spend those with her parents in Somerville. After all, they were paying a great deal for her medical education and that was the least she could do.

The following February, Bob was invited to the Red Sox spring training camp in Winter Haven, Florida. Although very excited at the opportunity to show off his skills, Bob realized that he was being reviewed by a team that had just lost the World Series in 1975 and, as an outfielder, would be up against three of the best active outfielders in the major leagues. He realized all the possible scenarios that could happen to him. If he did well in spring training, he might accompany the team back to Boston and serve as a substitute for any of the three outfield starters. As the team badly needed another starting pitcher, one of the starting outfielders might be traded for a top pitcher, opening the way for him to gain a starting role. Lastly, he himself might be traded as a top prospect to a team needing an outfielder. All of these things ran through Bob's mind as he prepared to leave Louisville in February of that year.

Bob decided to drive to Florida from Louisville and bid farewell to his parents and younger brother Ben a week before training camp began. By showing up early, Bob figured to make a good impression with the team management and, he did. Spring training went well and Bob's hitting and fielding impressed everyone including the fans. He was destined to stay with the team as they headed for the home season opener in April against the Detroit Tigers. His primary goal was to continue to improve in both the field and at the plate. This, he believed, would eventually get him into the starting lineup, if not with the Red Sox, with another team.

Passing the time away when not on the baseball field was something Bob never liked. Except for baseball, his life was empty without Julie. He would go for long walks along Commonwealth Avenue in Boston and would stop at Boston University's campus, find a quiet bench, and read books. He was not your typical jock.

On a very warm and humid day in July of that year, during one of the team's extended home stands, the Sox had an off day on a Thursday and Bob and his roommate decided to go to the Lenox Hotel bar on Boylston Street for a bite at lunch.

As they sat quietly at a table in the bar, he was startled by a voice from behind, "Hello Bob." To his surprise, there stood Julie, as beautiful as ever in a white medical jacket and carrying a pile of books. He rose so quickly that he almost stumbled, his heart beating so fast that he could feel it.

"Julie, is it really you, what are you doing here?" He didn't know whether to hug her, to kiss her or shake her hand, a very awkward moment from someone with so much self-confidence on the ball field. "What are you doing here?" he repeated. "Come sit down, tell me what's been happening with you. I didn't think I would ever hear from you or see you again." Before Julie could answer, the roommate rose from the table and told Bob that he had several errands to do and excused himself.

"I'm at B.U. med school now, Bob, transferred after my first year at Vanderbilt. My dad lost his job last year and Vanderbilt was just too expensive for him to handle, so I live at home in Somerville and commute here to B.U. I just finished my second year and start again in August with an internship at Mass. General while continuing here at B.U. My dad just got another job but I think I'll finish up here. B.U. has sort of grown on me and Massachusetts is still home to me. I missed not getting together at Christmas time like we had planned and I think of you all the time, my big baseball star. Where are you living? I was going to call your parents in Louisville and get your address here in Boston."

"You knew that I was playing for the Red Sox this year?" he asked.

"I may not be a jock like you, Bob, but anyone playing for the Red Sox gets talked about everywhere, even among medical students."

They sat at that table for hours until Julie mentioned that she had to get home for dinner because her parents were expecting her.

"Would you like to have dinner at our house tonight, Bob, or do you have other plans?" Julie asked.

"Well, I'll have to cancel my three dates for tonight, but I'd love to meet the rest of the Laflamme family again. Why don't we walk back to my place, or take a cab, it's only about a mile down on Boylston, and we can then take my car to Somerville. That way I can drive back later tonight."

CHAPTER 16

Julie and Bob were married in October of that year following the close of the baseball season. The Red Sox were not in any post-season play in 1976 but Bob's performance that year was sure to gain him a starting position the following spring. After a honeymoon in the Caribbean, Bob and Julie settled in a lovely house in Medway, away from the hectic pace of Boston.

In 1978, Julie received her medical degree and interned at Mass. General. While Bob's career in baseball continued to flourish over the next eight years, still with the Red Sox, Julie settled into a podiatry practice in the Medway community. In early 1987, at the Red Sox training camp in Florida, Bob suffered a broken collarbone when he crashed into the outfield wall chasing down a fly ball. Following extensive rehabilitation in the next four months, calcium deposits were detected in the injured arm forcing him to miss the entire season. After winning the American League in 1986 and being one strike away from winning the 1986 World Series, everything went wrong for the Red Sox in 1987, not just Bob Elliott's injury. After losing on opening day, the Sox never were in contention the whole year. Replacing Bob in the outfield was a newcomer and rising star, Luke Jones, along with several other rookies forced into starting roles due to other injuries on the team.

Now at age thirty-five, Bob Elliott's career was ending and in October of 1987, the Sox informed him that they would not renew his contract unless his arm strength was back to normal, something that Bob knew was unlikely to happen. Fortunately, Bob owned two restaurants in the area and had always wanted to spend more time developing wedding receptions and other high-class functions, as there were but a few restaurants large enough in the area to handle this type of business. In the off season, Bob had always spent a great deal of time at each location while still having a lot of free time to spend with Julie on ski trips and short vacations in warmer climates. Perhaps now would be the time to start a family, before Julie's biological clock ran out. The two had discussed this and were not shying away from moving forward. Bob's folks were wondering if they would ever be grandparents since Ben was not married yet and still lived in Louisville. He had followed in his father's footsteps as an engineer in the ceramics business for a local manufacturer.

The Elliotts from Louisville would visit New England each year at Thanksgiving, and this year was to be no different as Bob had planned for his parents and Ben to spend that week in Medway. In addition to the customary Thanksgiving dinner, there were tickets to the Patriots, Celtics, and Bruins squeezed in, as well as dinner at each of Bob's restaurants planned.

CHAPTER 17

Karl Pelland knocked on the door at 5 boulevard des Agneaux in Paris. The house was a three-story brick structure with three mailboxes outside.

"Bonjour, monsieur," Karl said to the elderly gentleman. "I am looking for a Mr. and Mrs. Elliott that once lived at this address in the '70s. Do you remember these people, monsieur? I am trying to locate them on an urgent matter."

"Americans. Carl Elliott was an American who lived here for just a year. Nice couple with a baby. I believe they went back to America, yes they had passage, I remember, on a ship," mentioned the elderly man, explaining that he owned the building and often corresponded with former tenants. The Elliotts were no different as Judy would send photos of Robert at least once a year following his birthday or as part of a family picture at Christmas.

"Would you have an address for the Elliotts?"

"Why should I give you their address, I do not even know who you are?"

Karl flashed his American Embassy card and explained that there were items that they were holding for the Elliotts from years before and the embassy just wanted to see if the Elliotts wanted these items returned to them, nothing serious but, if the embassy could not locate the family, the items would be thrown away, mostly records of their stay in France.

"The cards and pictures were stamped from Louisville, Kentucky, monsieur, that's all I know. I have not heard from them now in almost fifteen years. The boy in the pictures would not be a boy any longer, say about thirty-five years old or so. I did not know the second boy in the pictures later on, he was called Ben. I have the pictures, would you like to see them?"

* * *

The phone rang at Jim Howard's apartment in Providence at 9:00 p.m., 3:00 p.m. Paris time. An excited Karl Pelland was at the other end of the line.

"Jim, Karl here from Paris. The second kid's in the States, last address in Louisville, Kentucky. He's got a brother named Ben and his parents are Carl and Judy Elliott, gotta be in their sixties by now. I don't have any more on the kid, Robert Elliott, but I think you can take over from here since he's likely somewhere back there, maybe still in Louisville. Jim, another thing though, the old man in the building told me I was the second person asking about the Elliotts. The other guy was Arab-looking, wearing a dark suit, and speaking with a heavy foreign accent according to the old man who gave him the same information you're getting right now. Apparently, the Arab was very generous with the French francs for the old man."

"Holy shit, Karl, this is getting serious here. Okay, I'll take it from here. Thanks for your help and not a word to anyone about this."

"Right now, Jim, I don't even remember who you are, let alone these two kids. Good luck with this, I hope you find him before someone else does."

"Father Merrill, please," Jim said to the housekeeper answering the phone at St. Matthew's Rectory. Jim could hardly wait for Father Dick to come to the phone. After what seemed to be an eternity, he picked up the extension.

"Mr. Howard, you have news for me?" he queried.

"I have good news and bad news, Father. The good news is that we found both kids, one in Dijon and the other, believe it or not, back here in the United States, Louisville, Kentucky, I think. The bad news is that the one in Dijon, named Charles Larouche, a professor at the University of Bourgogne, was murdered three days ago and some Arab guy is hot on the trail for the second one, Robert Elliott, who may still be in Louisville. I'm flying out there first thing in the morning. I tried phoning them first, got their number through the operator in Kentucky, but there was no answer."

"Oh, my God, I can't believe this is happening," mumbled Father Dick as he collapsed in the lounge chair next to the telephone in his room. For several moments there was nothing but silence at both ends of the line.

"Father, Father Merrill, are you still there?"

"Mr. Howard, what can you tell me about Charles? Does he have a family—what happened?"

"My contact in Paris is mailing me the entire story as it appeared in the local paper in Dijon. I'll have the article translated and bring you a copy when I get back from Louisville. That's all I know right now, Father, but someone's looking to get rid of these guys real bad, and now there's only one left. I'll call you from Louisville if I can find him before someone else does. Sorry for being so abrupt, but I have some other things I need to do before flying out there and I need to make several more calls."

Father Dick was still in shock. First, after over thirty-five years, he finds out he is the father of two sons. Now, before he can even digest the information, he is informed that one was murdered and the other is in danger for his life wherever he is.

Charles Larouche and Robert Elliott, my sons, he pondered. A weird feeling came over him and he didn't know whether to feel remorse and anger on what was happening or no feelings at all. Father Dick just sat there staring aimlessly as if in a trance. This would be a long night.

At the breakfast table the following morning, following the seven o'clock Mass, Father Dick picked up the *Providence Journal* with his customary cup of coffee while the housekeeper prepared his usual eggs over easy with bacon and toast. On page 2, under the heading of World News, was the caption, *Eastern emirate to undergo surgery in US.* Father Dick read on, *The king of the small oil-rich Middle Eastern country of Khatamori, King Ahmad Maurier, will undergo a kidney transplant at Massachusetts General Hospital in Boston later this week. The king, age 68, has been suffering from progressive kidney failure for some time and was informed that a donor had been found. King Ahmad will be accompanied by his wife, Queen Farah, and an entourage scheduled to arrive in Boston today.*

"Bill, Father Dick here," said Father Dick on the phone to his long-time friend, Captain William Sullivan, in the Lincoln Police Department. "Say, an old acquaintance—once a prince and now a king of a small Middle Eastern country—is coming to Boston for surgery. It's been years since I've seen him and thought I'd visit him before his surgery to cheer him up. How would I find out what hotel he's staying at in Boston? His name is King Ahmad Maurier from a country called Khatamori."

"Father, I can see how that information might not be that easy to get, security and all, you know. Let me see what I can find out. My brother Tom still works for the Globe up there. Let me call you back."

"He may not be up there too long, Bill, so I'd appreciate anything you can do for me."

Thirty minutes later, Bill Sullivan returned the call and, through his brother's press connections, found out that the Mauriers were staying at the Westin Hotel at Copley Square. "As the royalty of a Middle Eastern oil country," Tom mentioned, "security is all over the place. There is no way anyone can get near the thirty-fifth floor where their suites are located."

Father Dick summoned his housekeeper and instructed her to reschedule any appointments he had for the day and informed her that he needed to go to Boston on an urgent matter. He ran to his quarters and threw a change of clothing into a valise along with his shaving kit. Within five minutes, he was out the rectory door and into his four-door Toyota Corolla headed toward Route 95 and downtown Boston, about an hour away. His hands began to sweat and he could feel perspiration across his forehead and on his body. What in the world was he doing? What would he say if he came face to face with Françoise, the Queen of Khatamori? What could he say, "Let's talk about the kids!"

Should he head directly to Mass. General or to the Westin? Was the operation today or tomorrow or whenever? Suppose it's already happened and it didn't go well? What could he say then? All these things ran through his mind that Tuesday morning in late November, just two days before Thanksgiving. He knew that he would need to be back at St. Matthew's by early Thanksgiving morning to say Mass. But right now that was the furthest thing from his mind.

The Corolla seemed to automatically take the exit toward Mass. General and he accepted that as being easier than trying to get to see Françoise in a highly guarded surrounding at the hotel. As he entered the main entrance to the hospital, he approached the reception desk and asked if the hospital chaplain was in. He explained that he was visiting Mass. General for the first time and wanted to introduce himself.

"I will page Father O'Malley for you. Who may I say is visiting?"

"Tell him, Father Richard Merrill from Rhode Island."

No sooner than Father Dick had plopped himself down in a chair in the reception area, a plump, red-cheeked priest headed directly toward him. "Father Merrill, is it now?" Father O'Malley asked with a smile. "I'm Sean O'Malley. Welcome to my parish among the sick. What brings you up to Mass. General, visiting a sick parishioner or relative?"

"No, Father, it's a little more complicated than that. Years ago, I befriended a young French girl who went on to become the Queen of Khatamori and she and her husband, King Ahmad Maurier, are scheduled to be here either today or tomorrow, but I don't know how to let her know that I'm here, what with all the security I'm sure will be around her husband."

"They're not here yet, Father; not until tomorrow. In the meantime, I'll make a few calls and see what I come up with. Where can I reach you?"

"Try the Westin Hotel. If I'm not there, call me at St. Matthew's Church in Lincoln, Rhode Island, four-oh-one, three-three-four, eight-six-three-two. I'm not sure if I can get a room at the Westin."

"If I can't reach you at either place, Father Merrill, I should be in my office near the chapel at six-one-seven, five-five-five, two thousand, extension five-five-six-two."

There was still time to see Françoise at the Westin today, Father Dick thought. Off he went headed for the hotel, not exactly sure yet just how he would get to see Françoise, but he would figure that out en route. Fifteen minutes later, he parked his car and entered the Westin heading straight for the front desk. Once there, he asked a clerk for paper and pen and an envelope with a message that he wanted delivered immediately to Queen Farah in her suite. Within minutes, a bellman was headed for an elevator. He inserted a special key just before punching the thirty-fifth floor button on the elevator. Father Dick then headed for the lounge and sat facing the bank of elevators and waited for what seemed like hours. As the note was handed to a member of the royalty's entourage, the bellman left. Within moments, the servant knocked on Queen Farah's bedroom door.

"A message for you, Your Highness. The hotel said the sender said it was urgent."

"Thank you, Kaleel, let me read it."

My dear Françoise,
I have news of the two boys. Must see you today.
I am downstairs in the Lobby Lounge.
Fr. Richard Merrill

Françoise scampered through the parlor area of the suite toward her husband's bedroom only to find his trusted personal assistant seated in a chair near the bedroom door.

"He is sleeping, Your Highness. I fear that the long journey from Khatamori has not been kind to him. He does not look well. Let us pray that the new kidney will be successful."

"I must leave briefly to meet an old friend in the lobby of the hotel."

"Your Highness, that is not wise and much too dangerous. We have enemies everywhere and it would be better if this old friend came to our suite instead where we have the local police stationed on the floor. Why not send Kaleel to the lobby to bring this friend here?"

"As you wish. Kaleel, the man is a priest by the name of Father Richard Merrill. I wish I could tell you more about what he looks like, but I have not seen him for many years. To be certain it is the right person, ask him the name of the French girl he once knew in Paris. He should answer

Françoise Dupont. Make certain he tells you the entire name."

Kaleel spotted Father Dick sitting in the lounge and immediately approached him with his instructions. Once Father Dick answered Kaleel's inquiry correctly, he was led to the elevators.

Father Dick accompanied Kaleel to the suite and, following a thorough frisking by the Boston police assigned to protect the royal family, was escorted into a huge parlor area where Father Dick was seated while the queen was informed of his arrival. Father Dick was again extremely nervous and no sooner than the servant had left the room, there appeared before him a beautiful woman garbed in fine silk robes and jewels, her head covered with a sheer veil and her blue eyes shining through like the radiance of the sky.

"May I present Queen Farah of Khatamori," bellowed Kaleel.

He jumped to his feet, his heart pounding just as it once did those many years ago when he first met her. He froze and did not know what to do.

"Hello, Richard, it is so nice to see you again after all these years."

"Hello, Françoise, I mean, Your Majesty. I am not certain that I would have known you."

"You will leave us now, Kaleel, and take the other servants with you. I will call you if I need you." Françoise asked Father Dick to sit and she sat on a sofa facing him.

"You are well, Richard?" Françoise inquired.

"As well as I could be under the circumstances, may I call you Françoise?" asked Father Dick.

"But of course, Richard, Ahmad still calls me Françoise and I only use the royal name of Queen Farah when I appear with Ahmad in public."

"It's not every day that a priest finds out he is the father of two sons after thirty-five years. This really came as a shock to me, and, at first, I wasn't going to do anything about it and thought about throwing your letter away. But then, how could I? After all, they are or were as much my sons as they were yours. I don't know that I would have done to them what you did, but I am not the one to judge. I only wish I had known sooner, although I don't know what I would have done different, maybe nothing at all. We were both so young."

"Richard, for years after I married Ahmad and we could not have children of our own, I wanted to tell him what had happened before I met him. But as each year passed, so did my willingness to do so. I do not know how he will react to this when I tell him tonight. He may die tomorrow, and I could not bear to see him going on his final journey without knowing the truth."

"Charles is dead, Françoise, murdered three days ago in Dijon by an intruder. His full name was Charles Larouche, and he was a professor at the University of Bourgogne in Dijon. The police have no suspect at this time. I have a good friend who is in Louisville, Kentucky, today and has a good lead on Robert, our other son. Robert Elliott was adopted by an American couple when they lived in Paris. As soon as I have more news on Robert, I will let you know. I hope to hear more tonight."

"It is as I had feared," exclaimed Françoise. "Answa is up to his deviousness and will stop at nothing to gain the throne if Ahmad dies. It is time to tell Ahmad everything.

How will your contact in Louisville get a message to you, Richard?" queried Françoise.

"I will call my housekeeper at St. Matthew's and leave the number of the hotel with her as soon as I get a room."

"If you are unable to get a room, you can stay in one of our rooms on this floor. I am certain we can make that happen. I cannot believe that a moment of love between us has caused such pain."

After a few moments of silence between them, Father Dick excused himself and headed back to the lobby. He was a man totally dejected. Ten minutes later he phoned Françoise's suite and left word he was in Room 911 and would be there all evening should the queen need to speak with him again that night.

CHAPTER 18

United Flight 88 landed at Standiford Field Airport in Louisville at 12:05 p.m. Jim had the written address of Carl Elliott from when he tried to telephone the Elliotts the previous night. He hailed a cab out front and twenty minutes later was outside 3265 Alta Vista Way. The cab pulled up to the curb outside the two-story Tudor style residence and Jim asked the driver to wait. He rang the front doorbell several times but no one answered. Jim crossed the lawn and spotted a neighbor in his garage fumbling with a rake and several leaf bags.

"Excuse me, sir, can you tell me if the Elliotts next door are away?" Jim asked with an anxious tone in his voice.

"Who wants to know?" retorted the cautious neighbor.

Jim reached inside his coat pocket and pulled out one of his insurance business cards. "Carl Elliott is the beneficiary of an insurance policy taken out with my company and I can't seem to reach him."

"Well, you came all the way from Rhode Island for nothing. Mr. Howard is it? The Elliotts are right next door to you in Massachusetts right about now. Every year they spend Thanksgiving with their son Bob in Medway. You know Bob Elliott, don't you, the Red Sox player?"

"Bob Elliott on the Red Sox is the son of Carl and Judy Elliott?" asked Jim in stunned disbelief.

"Sure is, though I think his career might be coming to an end soon, with all those injuries he's had in the last year. Who knows, he's not getting any younger."

"Thanks, I appreciate the time," Jim replied as he dashed back to the cab. "Back to the airport, and step on it, please."

It was only 2:00 p.m. when Jim reached the airport. He booked the next flight back to Providence—Delta 782 leaving Louisville at 3:10 p.m. and arriving in Providence at 6:05 p.m.— and headed for the nearest pay phone.

"Betty, Jim here. Listen, I'm on the road now but need a favor. I don't care how you do it, but I need an address in Medway, Massachusetts, for a Robert Elliott. The guy's the same Bob Elliott who plays for the Red Sox, so it might not be listed in too many places. Even if you have to drive to Medway to get his address from some local, do it. I must have that address today. I'll be in the office around six-thirty tonight. Please, Betty, this is very important, you might say even a life and death situation, and I'm not kidding you when I say that," Jim said to his secretary.

"I'll get right on it, Mr. Howard. I'll have that address on your desk one way or another."

"Thanks, and one last thing, get me the FBI's telephone number in Providence."

* * *

Harry Esten was a member of the Bureau in Providence and an old military buddy from Vietnam who served in the same unit with Jack Bumpus. He had gone to the FBI training school in Maryland right after the military and had been an agent ever since. When he checked his office that afternoon, Harry read a pink telephone slip left on his chair: "Meet me at the Gaslight Restaurant tonight around seven o'clock. It's urgent that I see you, Jim Howard."

"Oh, shit," Harry said, "there go my plans for an early night. What the hell is so urgent that he needs to see me tonight? What could be so important that can't wait 'til tomorrow morning, or couldn't he just call me, man, Thanksgiving is only a day away."

At 6:45 p.m., Jim arrived at his office in the Turks Head Tower. The night guard to the triangular twenty-story office building on the corner of Weybosset St. and Westminster St. recognized Jim and, after signing in at the guard station, Jim punched the fifteenth floor on the elevator. Hardly anyone would be in the office of Continental Life other than a few computer operators running off reports for use the next day. The note on his desk chair read: *Robert and Julie Elliott, 77 Tiffany Lane, Medway. Telephone is unlisted and no one in Medway knew it. If they did, they wouldn't give it to me. There were no other Elliotts even in the Medway phonebook. Happy Thanksgiving. Betty.*

Two streets over on Pine Street, Harry Esten ordered a Heineken at the Gaslight. The restaurant was small but well-decorated and a perfect place to meet someone for quiet conversation, good food, and excellent service. No sooner had Harry taken his first sip than Jim tapped him on the shoulder.

"Thanks for meeting with me, Harry, I need your help and I need it big," Jim announced with a somber look on his face. "I'm in over my head on something and this may be an issue for the FBI or the CIA or somebody like that."

They had the waiter usher them to a table in the far corner of the restaurant where no one was seated within three or four tables from them. Jim ordered a Southern Comfort Manhattan and he began to relate the entire story to Harry.

"Wow, Jim, how the hell did you get involved in all of this? I can see Major Bumpus getting into stuff like this, but you, no way."

"Who the hell do you think got me involved like this, Christ, Harry, Bumpus' saving my ass in 'Nam is coming back big time. I don't think he knows anything about this unless somehow Father Merrill has told him and he didn't mention it to me."

"Bob Elliott from the Red Sox is really the son of this Queen Farah or Françoise, the French girl that the priest gave his special blessing to all those years ago."

"It's all true, Harry, the other kid getting murdered earlier this week in Dijon and some suspicious Arab guy in Paris asking for some address for the Elliott family."

"Well, Jimmy boy, this can't wait too long. If we don't find Bob Elliott first, we may end up with egg on our faces that involves international consequences, even though it doesn't look that way at first glance."

Ahmad's trusted servant knocked on Françoise's bedroom door to announce that the king had just awoken and that the rest had been good for him. Françoise had been deep in thought over the last few hours on how she would break the news to him of her life before the Louvre. Ahmad had not met her parents until they attended the wedding ceremonies in Khatamori, but he had never engaged in any lengthy conversations with them. In the years following, both of Françoise's parents had passed away, her father in 1981 and her mother two years later.

She headed to Ahmad's quarters where he was attended to by a full-time nurse provided by Mass. General as a precaution before the transplant operation. She asked the nurse if she could speak to her husband alone. The nurse agreed, but said it was imperative that Ahmad's vital signs remain stable. Françoise said she understood and the nurse left the room.

She immediately went to his bedside and caressed him and asked how he was feeling.

"It would be nicer to be able to function normally at this time and, perhaps, tomorrow will be the beginning of a second life for us, Françoise. I would enjoy growing old with you."

"Tomorrow is a serious moment for you, my husband, and you know that the doctors are optimistic but cannot guarantee success in this operation. I do not know how I would live without you. You have been my life for all these years and we have always been honest with each other, something that has kept our marriage happy even though I could not give you children. I must finally tell you a story that you must hear, my dear Ahmad."

"What are you saying, Françoise?" queried Ahmad.

"I am saying that your cousin Answa is making sure that if anything should happen to you, that the kingdom will be his to rule. You will understand what I am saying when you hear my story."

Françoise turned away from Ahmad, stared out the window at the Boston skyline, and began. "When I was a young girl, several years before I met you at the Louvre, I conducted tours of Paris by bus for Le Bourse. While on one of these tours, I met a young American who was vacationing in Paris. He was the first person I made love to, but you have been the only other man I have shared my bed with. We were both very young and only on the night before he was to return to America did he reveal to me that he was a Catholic priest. I was very upset at this but, in time, the pain in my heart went away. A few months after he left, I found out that I was carrying his child. I was ashamed and confused and never told my parents. I secretly arranged to bear the child with the help of my landlady, who happened to be the sister of Claude Gagnon, the director at the Louvre. When the time came, I had two sons, Ahmad, two boys. I could not care for them; I could hardly care for myself since I had not worked for months. So I gave up the boys to an orphanage in Giverny for adoption. Today, the boys would be thirty-five years old, Ahmad, and I have never seen them in all that time. The problems I had giving birth to two babies are why I could never have more children, children that should have been by our side today."

"The father of these boys, he knows of them?" asked Ahmad in a quiet tone.

"Yes, I wrote to him a few weeks ago and asked him to help me find them. Our laws would allow them to succeed you in time, Ahmad, but I thought that no one else knew about them. The father's name is Father Richard Merrill and he was here in this hotel today to give me news. One of the boys was murdered in Dijon three days ago and the other is here somewhere in the United States, perhaps Louisville, Kentucky. Everything points to Answa as being behind this, and he will stop at nothing to gain the throne from you. Father Merrill is doing all he can to find the other son, Robert Elliott."

"I know of the orphanage, Françoise, I have always known. When one of my advisors asked me if I was going to give money to the orphanage each year, since he handled the transfer for you, I asked him to go there the next time business took him to France. It was not my wish to force you to tell me of this place and why you were sending money there, but I became aware that the money was going to two families. I married you, Françoise, for who you are, not for what or who you were before. If Answa is doing this, I will find out and deal with him, if I live to return to Khatamori."

"Now, did your son from Dijon have a family? If so, we must see to their well-being."

"No, Ahmad, he was not married."

"And when will we hear of the other son, this Robert Elliott?"

"Father Merrill said he would inform me as soon as he has news of him. He has taken a room here in the hotel."

"Perhaps at another time, I should like to meet this first love of yours."

* * *

Harry Esten picked up Jim Howard at his apartment on the east side of Providence at 8:00 a.m. on Wednesday and they headed for Medway via Route 495 to Route 126. Passing through the rural highway in Bellingham, there appeared to be a seamless connection between the two towns as they entered Medway, passing a restaurant, a colonial-styled bank, and several local stores. Harry pulled his car up to the curb on Main Street and he and Jim entered the Medway police station. Harry flashed his badge and asked to see the chief. Once formalities were addressed, Chief Oscar Anderson volunteered to escort the two of them to Tiffany Lane and the home of Bob Elliott.

Julie opened the front door after two rings and was somewhat surprised to see Chief Anderson there.

"Hello, Chief, Happy Thanksgiving. What brings you here this morning?" she asked.

"Is Bob at home, Julie, these two gentlemen are with the FBI and need to ask him a few questions, nothing serious, but he may be of some help to them in a case they're working on?"

"He went down to the restaurant to go over some things with the staff. We expect a pretty good crowd for lunch and dinner on Thanksgiving and, well, you know Bob, he wants to make sure there are no surprises. Is there something I can do to help?"

"Not a problem, Julie, we'll just go down to the Lamplighter and see him there. No need to call him either, Julie, I wouldn't want you to get him worried for nothing. But I'm going to leave a squad car out front, just in case we miss him at the restaurant; that way the officer can just radio me when Bob gets back here. Have a nice day, Julie."

The Lamplighter was on Route 126 heading back toward Bellingham. Harry Esten's car followed the Medway Police vehicle there. As they entered the parking lot adjacent to the front door of the restaurant, Chief Anderson noticed Bob's car parked near the side entrance. Before Anderson led Harry and Jim to the entrance, Harry pulled Anderson aside and asked him to keep the police car in front of the Elliott residence for security reasons. He explained to Anderson that there might be a threat on Bob Elliott's life and the FBI did not want to take chances. Anderson agreed and left.

Harry and Jim entered the restaurant and were greeted by a tall, blond good looking man with a broad smile.

"Good morning, gentlemen, I'm afraid we are not open at this time of day. Is there something I can help you with?"

"Yes, you're Bob Elliott, aren't you? I recognize you from your Red Sox pictures."

"Yes, how can I help you?"

"Mr. Elliott, my name is Harry Esten from the Providence office of the FBI and this is Jim Howard, an acquaintance of mine in Rhode Island. We believe there is a serious threat on your life. It appears that it has nothing to do with you directly but more to do with your birth history. Are you familiar with your birth, Mr. Elliott?"

"I know I was adopted as a baby, if that's what you mean, I don't know much more about it than I was born in Paris," Bob answered. "What is this all about?"

From the front entranceway, Jim noticed a black sedan parked directly across the street from the restaurant. There were two men in the car and they were just sitting there. Jim immediately tapped Harry on the shoulder and pointed to the vehicle across the street.

"Mr. Elliott, please stay inside. Whatever you do, do not leave the restaurant unless one of us comes back for you, understood?" Harry's voice was loud and crisp in his message. "If you see anyone else even heading for the front door, head out the side to your car and go straight to the police station. First, make sure the doors are locked as well. Go now, please."

"Jim, you'd better not get too close to me. If those guys are armed, you'll be a sitting duck," Harry shouted as he headed out the front door with his gun drawn.

The dark sedan's engine suddenly started and, the car made a quick U-turn in the restaurant parking lot. The passenger window rolled down and bullets came rapidly toward Harry, several smashing the glass on the front door behind him. Lucky for Harry, none of the shots hit him or Jim who was several feet behind. Harry threw himself to the ground and began firing at the speeding car as it headed back toward Medway.

Harry rose and dusted himself off. He kept repeating H6254. He reached into his coat pocket and jotted the number down on his pad. Almost simultaneously, he dashed for his car and grabbed the car phone on the floor and called in the license plate number. In non-stop fashion, he called the Medway police station to alert them of the vehicle and to be sure that protection was maintained at the Elliott house. Chief Anderson assured him that an APB on the car would be sent immediately to all squad cars in the area and in surrounding towns. Harry left his car phone number with Anderson and asked him to let him know as soon as he got information on the car.

Within minutes, Harry's phone rang and it was Anderson on the other end of the line. "Mr. Esten, the car is a rental from Hertz out of Logan and we're on the phone with them now to see who rented the car. Hang on a minute," an excited Anderson bellowed. "I've got it now: the car was rented by a Fajid Singh, it's a foreign license and they're faxing a copy of it to us now. Don't leave the restaurant, stay put—I'll have somebody there in five minutes."

"Okay, Chief, will do. Jim, get back inside and make sure the others stay there too, and lock all the other doors. I'll be in in a minute."

Harry picked up the phone and contacted the Boston FBI office for more information. He instructed them to check with Logan Airport on all arrivals from Kentucky in the last two days and to get passenger lists for them to review to see if Fajid Singh's name appeared or other Arab names on the same flight. He then asked the Boston office to get him all the information they had on Singh in their files or through the CIA. He would fax them a copy of the license as soon as he saw it from the Medway police.

Inside the restaurant, Jim was impressed at how quickly Harry reacted to this situation and the calmness with which he went about his business. Harry was a trained professional and this incident was not to be taken lightly. Within hours, the area would be crawling with agents from both Boston and Providence, along with local police, looking for a 1987 black Chevrolet Impala with Massachusetts license plate H6254.

In the meantime, calls were made to all area motels and hotels to find out if two Arab men had checked in together recently. The process would be tedious because there are many hotels and motels within a twenty-mile radius of Medway. If this turned up nothing, the search would be expanded to include places in Boston near Logan airport.

As the minutes passed, Jim could see the fright on Bob Elliott's face as he was hunched over behind the maître d' station, out of vision from the front door.

"I don't understand this," he shouted. "What's going on here?"

After cautiously looking out the shattered glass door in the front of the restaurant, Jim moved quickly toward Bob to reassure him that everything would be okay.

"It's complicated, Mr. Elliott," Jim began, "but it seems that the woman who gave you up for adoption in Paris later married a prince from a Middle Eastern oil country and later became king when his father died. Any son of the king or queen, your birth mother, can become the next king if her husband dies. You were a twin, Mr. Elliott, and your twin brother was murdered four days ago in France. There are some mean guys out there who don't want either of you to be in line to succeed the king."

"Succeed a king," queried Bob frantically, "are you out of your fucking mind? All I know is my parents who raised me. I don't give a shit about an Arab oil country."

"I know it's hard to swallow, but that doesn't mean anything to these guys. They're hired to eliminate the possibility of a successor, period, and that's now you and you alone," Jim replied.

Within minutes, Chief Anderson's police car arrived at the Lamplighter and he was shocked at the bullet-laden holes at the entrance of the restaurant. Another Medway police cruiser arrived and Bob Elliott was carefully escorted into Anderson's car. The two cruisers then headed back to Bob's house on Tiffany Lane where other cruisers were congregating at curbside in front of the residence. Harry had indicated that Bob's car would first be thoroughly searched for any explosive device and then would be driven to his home once the inspection was complete.

After Anderson had handed Harry a faxed photo of Singh's driver's license, Harry had instructed Bob not to leave his home until further notice. He asked Anderson to place a perimeter of officers completely around the Elliott property. Harry said he would meet with them shortly as he and Jim needed to wait for more information first.

After making a call to St. Matthew's to inform Father Dick of the recent events, Jim was given his telephone number at the Westin.

"Father Merrill, Jim Howard, I have news on Bob Elliott. He is the same Bob Elliott who plays for the Red Sox and he lives in Medway. His parents are the ones who live in Kentucky but they spend the Thanksgiving weekend at Bob's house every year. That's the good news, Father," Jim explained.

"No, oh no, Mr. Howard, please don't tell me something bad has happened to him too," Father Dick said in disbelief.

"No, he's alive. Someone tried to shoot him this morning, but the FBI is in on this now and were able to stop the guys this time. It's a very scary situation here, but the police are protecting him and his family until they can catch these guys. It looks like the same people who were in Dijon earlier this week. By the way, what are you doing in Boston, anyway?" asked Jim.

Father Dick explained his meeting Françoise and about her husband's scheduled kidney transplant operation the day after Thanksgiving. Apparently, Harry had already informed the Boston FBI office to increase the security at the hotel. He also asked that the Bureau add security at Mass. General in anticipation of Ahmad's arrival there on Friday morning.

Around noon on Wednesday, Harry received a fax at the Medway police station with more information on Fajid Singh.

Fajid Singh, a.k.a. Saad Al Abdullah, is a known and hunted assassin from Saudi Arabia according to a CIA dossier. Singh is credited with several killings of Middle Eastern members of the royal family in Qatar, where the ruling party was in conflict with military leaders attempting a coup. Singh is known to team up with Abou Ben Habib, another CIA watch. Singh rented a car in Paris for two days last Saturday. Both men were listed as passengers on a flight from Paris to Louisville under the names of Said Mushtaf along with Habib under the name of Muhammad Desai. Tuesday's Delta flight from Louisville to Logan Airport showed both of them arriving in Boston yesterday. Both are considered armed and extremely dangerous.

Harry and Jim left the police station and headed for the Elliott household. Carl Elliott answered the doorbell and, after flashing the official formalities, he showed them into the living room off the main foyer. Bob Elliott's house was huge and the first level was ideally suited for social gatherings with a large L-shaped living room, complete with fireplace and Steinway in opposite corners and surrounded with several soft chairs on a thick beige carpet. The L-shape led into a large dining room with a table surrounded by ten chairs and a very large hutch set between a side and rear window. It was much too visible from the outside Harry observed. The dining room, in turn, led into a lively kitchen area bright with natural sunlight reflecting through sliding doors leading to a patio that ran the length of the kitchen and dining rooms and accessible from both rooms. The remainder of the first floor consisted of a large family room connecting to a screened-in porch which also led to the rear patio. Bob and Julie were seated in the living room along with Ben and Judy.

Harry briefed everyone on the latest developments but soundly warned all family members that the danger remained as the two assailants were still at large. Guards were posted on all sides of the house until further notice. Bob was still stunned from the morning gunshots and attempt on his life. He had difficulty understanding why this was happening to him. His father, Carl, was also perplexed and tried to console the family as best he could. The news of a queen being the natural mother to his adopted son was so bizarre that he too did not know how to react to this revelation.

"I'll let Jim Howard try to fill you in on exactly what has happened here," lamented Harry almost with an apologetic tone. Jim related the entire story from the beginning and, except for not identifying Father Dick by name, recounted the brief encounter in Paris nearly thirty-six years earlier. The eventual transition of Françoise Dupont into a princess and, subsequently, a queen of an oil-rich country was right out of a fairy tale. Were it not for the allowance of heirs to the monarchy from either spouse, none of this conspiracy would be occurring. Jim informed everyone of the king's upcoming surgery in Boston and that the natural father also was in Boston. He further related how the priest had never been aware of any pregnancy and eventual birth of two sons until a week earlier and that is how he had become involved in the sequence of events.

"I have another brother," Bob said.

"I'm afraid to let you know, Mr. Elliott, that he was killed by what we believe to be the same two people looking for you right now and at the restaurant this morning. Your natural brother, and twin, was a college professor in France and his name was Charles Larouche, a bachelor. The murder was meant to look like a break-in, but, given all that's happened in the last few days, we're convinced that these people are the same ones we traced from France."

CHAPTER 19

Thanksgiving morning at the Elliotts was not the customary early rising in preparation for breakfast at Danny's Diner in Medway and the traditional high school football game between Medway and Millis that followed. Instead, the family quietly gathered in the kitchen and dining room for coffee and an assortment of cereals, muffins, and fruit, courtesy of the Medway Police Department. Bob, over the years, had always been supportive of the police union and provided autographed baseballs each year as part of the fund raiser for the policemen's emergency fund. A police officer, standing guard outside their front door, brought in the morning newspapers and indicated that he would do the same the following day along with any mail delivered to their mailbox.

Every member of the family was now in the position of keeping themselves busy under the house confinement orders by the FBI. Windows had been covered in dark cloth to prevent any view of the family inside the house. Unfortunately, this also prevented any daylight from entering except for two skylights in the ceiling of the screened porch. Bob offered the officers coffee several times but was told that they were fine and were often relieved by other police officers since the weather that morning was only in the 20s, much colder than normal for Thanksgiving.

Chief Anderson had been able to get a local glass dealer to replace the glass broken by the gunfire at the Lamplighter. The restaurant had hundreds of lunch and late afternoon reservations on Thanksgiving and closing the restaurant would have imposed too much hardship on the patrons of the establishment. Bob had thought about closing the Lamplighter due to the shooting, but as it turned out, it would be dinner as scheduled thanks to Chief Anderson. It was Bob's intention to keep the Wednesday episode quiet and all employees had been ordered to do the same. Bob's maître d' would operate the Lamplighter on Thanksgiving in his absence. He had called the restaurant at 11:00 a.m. to make sure that all the proper arrangements had been made as patrons would begin arriving around 11:30 a.m. for the Noon seating. There would also be a 2:00 p.m. and 4:00 p.m. seating to follow.

Bob still had a lot of difficulty understanding what was going on and how, suddenly, his secure lifestyle was threatened by something completely out of his control.

At the Westin Hotel in Boston, Ahmad and Françoise were spending a quiet day in their suite along with other members of the king's entourage. Security in and around the hotel had been heightened and no one was allowed access to the thirty-fifth floor unless previously approved by the king himself or by Françoise. Father Dick had left early that morning to say Thanksgiving Mass in Rhode Island and planned to return to Boston later that same day. He had informed Françoise that he would call immediately if there was word from the FBI on the two assassins. By now, the state police had joined the manhunt for Singh and DeSai, and all agencies had full descriptions of the two assailants and the vehicle they were driving. Somehow, they had eluded the search and were nowhere to be found.

Ahmad was angry at the thought that a relative would plot against the succession laws of Khatamori, but more so that it was Answa, whom he felt closer to than anyone except Françoise. Apparently the Minister of Finance had also innocently informed Answa of the series of payments that had been made years before by Françoise to the orphanage in Giverny. The Minister felt that, in the event these payments required further investigation, the head of the country's security should be made aware.

The telephone in Ahmad's suite rang and it startled Françoise considering the circumstances with the assassins on the loose and the impending surgery to Ahmad on Friday. The king's servant answered and immediately looked at Ahmad.

"It is the long-distance operator, Your Majesty."

"This is Ahmad Maurier, you have a call ready for me?" he queried.

"Mr. Maurier, we have a Mr. Arif on the line, one moment please."

"Hello, Your Majesty?"

"Kirit, I have some very important instructions for you. You are to arrest Answa immediately and see to it that his confinement is well guarded. You are also to take the military guard and surround the entire palace grounds until I or the queen tell you otherwise. I fear that Answa has betrayed us, but I cannot be certain yet. Is that clear?" Ahmad's voice was getting louder, so much so that the assigned nurse outside his bedroom door burst in at the loud voice.

Ahmad noticed the concerned look on her face and immediately held the phone aside and told her, "I'm sorry for the loudness, I am on a long-distance call and thought that speaking louder would help. There is nothing to be alarmed about," he continued.

"Your Majesty, you must remain calm, it is crucial that your vital signs remain normal before and up to the time of the transplant operation," the nurse replied.

"Yes, yes, I know, I will be sure that it does not happen again," he assured her and she hesitantly left the room.

"Kirit, did you understand what I just told you?"

"Yes, Your Majesty, your orders will be carried out at once."

Kirit Arif was the Minister of Defense which, in such a small country, amounted to a mere two hundred soldiers that guarded the borders and served as honor guards at functions in the palace. Kirit was loyal and trustworthy and did not question the reasons for the orders, he would just follow them. Ahmad told Kirit to call him back immediately once Answa was under house arrest.

At nearly the same time, Singh was calling Answa to inform him about what had happened at the restaurant. When Answa answered, he was concerned that the

American authorities were on to them and that it would be nearly impossible to get near Bob Elliott at this time.

"Fajid, I want you to kill Habib. Remove your hair and mustache, and buy a pair of glasses to change your appearance. They are looking for two men, not one. Use a different name; say a French name, not a Muslim one that would attract too much attention. Get rid of the car and steal another. So many cars are stolen in the United States that another will not make anyone connect it to you. Once you have done this, you are to rent a furnished apartment in the town near where Bob Elliott lives. In a few days, security will not be so strict. Am I clear?"

"Yes, Answa, he is right here in the room with me, I will take care of it," Singh replied.

"I will leave immediately for America and contact you when I arrive. Be at the North Central Airport in Lincoln, Rhode Island, on Saturday. I will be arriving there in the afternoon. We may need to take care of Ahmad first. The Elliott son can wait for now."

"Remember, Fajid, I need someone like you to head my security force after this is over."

"I will be there, Answa, er, we will be there," Singh muttered as Habib was looking at the television while stretched out on the bed in the motel room. There is no honor among assassins. Shortly there would be only one.

Habib never knew what hit him as the two bullets from the silencer killed him instantly. Singh would dispose of his body that night, check out of the motel, and leave the rental car in a parking lot in another town, miles away. Stealing another car would not be difficult as he positioned himself near an all-night convenience store where customers would leave their keys in the ignition as they picked up a few items. Oftentimes, they even left the motor running as they never suspected that they would be victimized in such a short time.

Singh shaved his head, beard, and mustache and had bought a pair of cheap eyeglasses at a local drugstore in Woonsocket, twenty minutes away from Medway. He had left the rental car in a supermarket parking lot where it would not likely attract attention for several days. Habib's body was rolled in bed sheets and stuffed in the trunk.

Thanksgiving night was cold in Rhode Island with temperatures dipping into the low 20s. When the '86 Chevy Impala pulled up to the L'Il General convenience store, Singh was positioned at the side of the building as he watched the man enter the store, his car engine still emitting smoke from the November chill. He made a beeline for the car and, in a split moment, sped down the road unnoticed. He entered Bellingham on Route 126 and stopped at the first market he found, picked up a local newspaper, and went next door to the Pinecrest Diner. While there, warming up over a bowl of soup, Singh scoured the want ads for furnished apartments and found several. He managed to get one that night and decided to lay low over the next day until Answa arrived at North Central on Saturday.

In the meantime, Ahmad received a second call from Kirit informing him that Answa had been arrested and confined to his quarters in Khatamori. Answa vehemently denied any wrongdoing and was furious at Ahmad's orders to arrest him. Following this news, Ahmad wrote a message in which he asked Kirit to relay to Answa. It read:

I will deal with you upon my return home. Kirit will confine you to your quarters until

I return. Should any harm come to Robert Elliott, Kirit has been instructed to execute you upon hearing such news. You are to remove your butchers, Singh and Habib, from the United States at once. I had expected more from you, my cousin. Ahmad

As Jim Howard was about to leave Medway and head back to Providence late that afternoon, Harry arranged for one of the local police cruisers to give Jim a ride back as Harry's job was clearly not over, not by a long shot. Both of them were outside the front of the Elliott residence when a car slowly approached the property, its headlights glaring in the distance, alerting several policemen to draw their weapons as they crouched behind two cruisers in front of the house. The car slowed down quickly until it came to a complete stop several hundred feet from the Elliott driveway.

"Place your hands where we can see them and get out of the car slowly," blasted the police speaker.

The figure complied with the request and there in the darkness stood Father Dick, in his black suit with Roman collar, hands raised.

Jim yelled to the police, "Don't fire, I know this man, he is not a threat."

"Mr. Howard, I'm sorry to alarm anyone. I was on my way back to the Westin and somehow could not help but see if I could meet Bob Elliott. I am worried for his safety, and I feel responsible for all of this and, well, he is my son."

"You really should have called me, Father, I'm not sure that this is the right time for this," Jim replied. "You could have gotten killed here; no one else even knows what you look like but me."

"You're right, of course, I didn't think of that. I just had to do this, Mr. Howard. Do you think Bob Elliott would meet with me, even for just a few minutes, please?"

The look of anguish on Father Dick's face was more than Jim could bear. Here was a man whose secure life, as it had been, was now completely turned upside down. His years of devotion to the church had suddenly been overshadowed by an innocent youthful tryst so long ago that he barely remembered it happening. His one and only sexual encounter amid a celibate life since then had resulted in two sons, one murdered and the other under threat of a similar fate. How could he know how to handle this situation, how does one confront a thirty-five year old son he has never seen nor even known about?

Jim rang the doorbell and Julie answered. The Elliotts had eaten their customary 4:00 p.m. Thanksgiving dinner and were quietly sipping coffee and after-dinner drinks as they sat in the living room.

"Mr. Howard, you have more news, have they caught those men?" Julie asked eagerly.

"No, ma'am, not yet. I am here because of an unusual request. Do you recall that I told you that Bob's real father was a young priest at the time he had the affair in Paris?" Jim continued. "Well, he is here, right outside, and wants to meet Bob if he can, even if only for a minute."

"I can't speak for my husband, Mr. Howard, but I will pass this along to him and let him decide if he wants to do this right now or not. You really know how to foul up our lives, don't you? No, no, I'm sorry, Mr. Howard, this is not your fault, it's only that this is amazing news and quite bizarre, don't you think?"

"Yes, ma'am, it's very bizarre indeed. I'll just wait outside while you talk this over with Bob." He headed down the front walk toward the cruisers and Father Dick standing there with Harry.

Ten minutes later, the front door opened and Julie motioned to Jim to come up. Bob had agreed to meet Father Dick if only to see his face, but the meeting would be held with all family members, not just Bob. Bob had nothing to hide and everyone in the family had a right to know the face behind the story.

As Father Dick entered the front hallway, he introduced himself to Julie and thanked her for the opportunity to meet Bob.

Julie escorted him into the living room and announced, "Everyone, this is Father Richard Merrill, Bob's birth father." The silence was deafening.

"Hello, Father Merrill. I'm Bob Elliott and this is my family," chimed in Bob as he made the rounds introducing the other family members. Carl was not pleased at meeting Father Dick and Bob's mother, Judy, would not even look his way. Ben thought this was cool, adding excitement to a normally quiet weekend in Massachusetts.

"Please be seated, Father. Can I get you something to drink?" motioned Julie.

"No, I'm fine thank you. I'm very sorry for interrupting your holiday and for disrupting your lives. I wish none of this ever happened, but it did. Years ago, I made a foolish decision as a young priest on holiday in a foreign country. I never realized that any of this would be happening and that evil people would seek harm to either of the two boys. Obviously, with one of them already dead, God rest his soul, I am now paying the price for that decision.

Bob, I am your natural father but there is no way that I could replace the love and sacrifice that your parents have made over the years in raising you. But I thought you should know at least who I am, that's all. Your birth mother's name was Françoise Dupont and, long after she gave you and your brother up for adoption, she married Prince Ahmad Maurier of Khatamori, a small but very rich Middle Eastern oil country. Apparently, the birth of twins early on had prevented Françoise from having more children later on. As you can well imagine, a kingdom needs heirs and the Mauriers had no children of their own. But Françoise, who is now Queen Farah, had two boys and, according to the custom in Khatamori, they are eligible to succeed the throne now held by Ahmad. You may have read recently that he is in Boston for a kidney transplant tomorrow morning. If he does not recover, the country has a succession problem with Françoise the only remaining living Maurier, except for the king's cousin who appears to be behind all of this in an effort to secure the crown for himself. He is thought to be responsible for the death of your natural brother, Charles Larouche, in Dijon last week."

Father Dick continued, "Françoise is a good queen from what I'm told and extremely loyal to her husband. For years, she sent money to your parents through the orphanage so that you would never be wanting. Even if and when they catch these criminals, I don't know how this will get settled."

"Father, as far as I'm concerned, there's nothing to settle," Bob interrupted, "I just want my life to go on normally and raise my own family while we have the chance to. I don't care about Katamanga, or whatever this place is called, and I particularly don't care about you or the queen one way or the other. I don't want to be the heir of a throne, so if something happens to the king, that's not my problem. I just don't like the idea of somebody shooting at me, would you?" Bob was bitter at the situation his family had been put in and abruptly rose to his feet and faced Father Dick.

"Thank you for coming, Father, but I don't believe we have anything further to say to each other."

The trip back to the Westin would wear heavily on Father Dick as he left the Elliotts and drove his car back onto Route 95 to Boston.

"I'm sorry for the outburst," Bob began in front of his family, "but, even though I knew about being adopted in France from unknown parents, I guess I just wasn't ready or expected to hear about my birth parents in this way."

He hugged his parents and broke down in tears.

CHAPTER 20

Answa's quarters on the outskirts of Banra were quite an elaborate mini-palace of its own. As a prominent dignitary in Khatamori, and the only cousin to King Ahmad, he was wealthy in his own right, sharing part of the oil fortune in the Maurier family. Wealth, in this case, did not mean power, at least not the kind of power that comes with ruling a country.

Answa had asked Kirit to be confined in his library and Kirit saw no reason to deny him that request. Guards would be placed outside the library entrance and on the grounds over Answa's entire property. As Kirit was about to leave Answa in his library, Answa poured himself a tall brandy and asked Kirit if he would join him. The sneer on his face angered Kirit, speeding his exit from the room as he slammed the door as he left. Answa could hear noise at the door, realizing full well that the guards were barricading him inside.

At almost the same time, Answa quickly drew the curtains on his windows, isolating himself from any view outside. He walked to a bookcase and grabbed the wall lamp adjacent to it and twisted it sideways and back. Immediately, one section of the bookcase popped open revealing a passageway behind the wall. Answa entered the passageway and turned on a light switch as he shut the bookcase behind him. In the passageway, a safe contained a vast amount of American dollars, a pistol, a passport and other papers he would need. He had prepared himself for such an event. A good security officer always prepares himself for his own security, he thought. The passageway led to an underground tunnel that went completely outside his palace grounds where a loyal servant laid waiting in an old automobile, one that would not attract attention as it made its way toward a private airstrip at the farther side of Banra. Answa had access to the royal family's Falcon jet and boarded virtually unnoticed. It would be hours before anyone realized that he was gone from his confinement. Once Kirit realized that the Falcon jet was gone, there would be no way to trace his whereabouts. He would be on his way to the United States. Captain Ed Kocon, the king's personal pilot, had earlier been taken at gunpoint to the airstrip from his quarters a few miles away.

Security outside the royal suite at the Westin had again been increased following the receipt of the telegram from Kirit.

Answa has escaped using secret tunnel in his quarters/Stop/ Falcon jet also missing/Stop/Beware as I fear he is heading for the US/Stop/Kirit.

The FBI had been notified and immediately took action. All air traffic control towers were alerted to notify the FBI of any incoming flights from foreign soil attempting to land at their airport. Additional agents were assigned at the Elliott home in Medway and the Maurier suite in Boston. Harry had a suspicion that the king was going to be more vulnerable to intruders in a place like Mass. General following his planned surgery on Friday. Since there were adequate security officers guarding the Elliotts, he decided to head for Boston to help in the protection of the king and queen.

Traffic to Boston late in the day on the holiday was light as most people also had Friday off from work and there were no major activities going on in Boston on Thanksgiving night.

The Bureau had taken space on both the twenty-ninth and thirtieth floors of the Westin and had positioned agents at all staircases on each floor, including the thirty-fifth. Harry knocked on the door of the royal suite and was greeted by a fellow agent. Once inside, he asked to speak to Ahmad and Françoise. After introducing himself to them, he updated them on the status of the two assassins and about the brief meeting that Father Merrill had with the Elliotts earlier that evening. Harry believed that Father Merrill was back in his room at the Westin and would likely call to inform them of what had transpired in Medway. He informed the royal family of the security net that had been put in place to prevent Answa from penetrating the area, should he make such an attempt. Ahmad chuckled at this news and alerted Harry at how clever and resourceful Answa was in eluding people when he had to.

"You cannot capture what you cannot find," continued Ahmad, "and Answa will not allow himself to be captured unless he chooses to be captured. He would die first, that is the type of man you are dealing with. He will change how he looks, how he walks and speaks, and how he dresses to elude authorities. What I do not know is how many people he will have with him."

"I understand, Your Highness, and," Harry continued, "we will do everything in our power to see to it that you and the queen are not in any danger."

Harry bid the two good night and wished the king success in his operation the next morning. Harry would be stationed in a room on the thirty-fourth floor, directly below the king's suite.

The phone rang again in the royal suite and Father Dick asked to speak to Françoise. He told her of his meeting with Bob Elliott and the bitterness that Bob held toward him and Françoise for disrupting his life and placing his family in danger. Françoise took the news very badly and nearly broke down on the telephone conversation. She hoped that there would be an opportunity to calm this animosity in Bob when the whole affair was over. She too realized how her actions years before now came back to torment her. What could possibly make this right, she wondered.

Realizing that the following morning would be nerve-wracking enough for Françoise, Father Dick inquired if it would be all right to sit with her in the waiting room during the operation on Friday. Françoise, who had been a devout Catholic in her younger days, agreed to this and would inform the authorities at the hospital to allow him into the private waiting area that was near the recovery room at the hospital. Friday would be a very long day as the transplant surgery was expected to take at least five hours.

Ahmad called Françoise by his bedside and began to speak in a very soft voice. "If tomorrow does not go well, I will be with my father and you will be the one who must keep the peace in Khatamori and care for our people. If Robert Elliott wants no part of us, then his name must never be revealed after Answa is dealt with. You cannot allow these people to fear living in the face of threats on their lives. Whether I live or die, you must meet this child of yours and make peace with having abandoned him so many years ago. I do not want you to forget your child, but there are so many other children that you can help now, perhaps they all can be the children we never had. I hope to be with you again, Françoise, if not tomorrow, then in the next kingdom where my father dwells. And now, I must sleep, my beloved queen. May Allah guide you on your journey as I pray he will on mine."

At 9:00 p.m., the nurse entered Ahmad's bedroom to administer a sleeping aid to him. At 5:00 a.m. the next day, Ahmad would be transported by ambulance to Mass. General for prepping work prior to the scheduled 8:00 a.m. operation. Ahmad, almost instantly, fell into a deep sleep.

Five a.m. came quickly and, as the ambulance technicians arrived at the hotel, the FBI agents searched them thoroughly as well as the ambulance itself. Agents had been assigned in three separate cars to escort the ambulance to Mass. General. Harry would be in the third car, behind the ambulance, while the other two vehicles would be in front of the ambulance. At the hospital, an equal number of Boston policemen were stationed at the emergency entrance while several other police officers were scattered at different stairwells throughout the hospital.

Ahmad arrived at the hospital at 5:15 a.m. and was led to the operating room prepping area. The hospital staff on duty was uneasy at all the security in and around the area but went about their business as best they could. Ahmad was lightly sedated but constantly held Françoise's hand in the prep room. At 7:30 a.m., a team of doctors, dressed in full operating room gowns and masks, entered the room for a final check on all of Ahmad's vital signs. The next time Ahmad would see them again, God-willing, would be in the recovery room several hours after the surgery.

Françoise was led into the private waiting area where Father Dick had already arrived. She greeted him with a faint smile, one of concern written all over it. He had a prayer book in his left hand as he clasped Françoise's two hands into his. Both sat quietly in the room for several minutes before Françoise spoke first.

"I was young, Richard, even younger than you that year in Paris. If I had never had your children, I probably would never have had the chance to work at the Louvre and meet Ahmad. He is my life, Richard, and I ask you to pray with me today as I have not prayed in a long time for his life."

"All of this is my fault, Françoise, not yours. You had no way of knowing that I was a priest and I had no right to deceive you. I have asked for God's forgiveness so many times over the years, but never more than now when I realize what I have done to two innocent lives, the boys I never knew," lamented Father Dick. "I, too, have been blessed with many years of happiness as a priest and do not wish anything but good health to your husband and our only remaining son. Robert Elliott is a fine man and his parents have brought him up well. But, first, let us talk more about your husband."

Françoise and Father Dick began a peaceful and lengthy conversation about their life experiences since Paris, and this served to calm them both.

At 1:30 p.m., a doctor appeared in the waiting room to inform Françoise that the operation and transplant were over and that everything appeared to have gone well. Ahmad would spend several days in recovery under strict observation for rejection symptoms that normally occur following transplants. Françoise asked to see him and the doctor indicated that she could only do so through a glass doorway as it was imperative that the recovery area remain virtually sterile.

Father Dick, in the meantime, was heading out the room on his way to the chapel on another floor when Françoise asked him to accompany her to the viewing area. He was pleased to do this and it felt comforting to both of them.

Through the glass windows, Ahmad was connected to an array of tubes and monitors, with a nurse seated in the room alongside him. Two of the surgeons were on call and only a phone call away should there be any complications that arose. Françoise touched the window gently, as if reaching to make contact with Ahmad, tears flowing down her cheeks. Father Dick led her away to a separate suite that had been prepared for her as she had indicated that she would not leave the hospital without Ahmad, one way or another.

Father Dick excused himself after insisting that she get some rest. He headed for the chapel following a stop for coffee in the hospital cafeteria. He had offered to return to her suite in a few hours and left the extension of the hospital chaplain where he could be reached. She was grateful at his kindness and it brought back memories of thirty-five years earlier when she first met him on that bus in Paris. So many years had passed and, yet, she felt as if she knew him well.

CHAPTER 21

Captain Kocon, the pilot for the royal family's jet, under gunpoint, was told to call the tower at North Central Airport to make an emergency landing there due to engine problems.

"This is Falcon Jet K-three-four-oh from Bangor requesting an emergency landing due to engine malfunction."

The air traffic controller asked the pilot for identification and whether he was carrying any passengers and crew. The pilot, an American airman now flying the Maurier's plane on a regular basis, was familiar with the routine necessary under emergency conditions. Answa had told the pilot to identify the aircraft as from a city in the United States so as not to arouse suspicion in the event authorities were on the alert for a foreign plane entering the US skies. The Falcon had flown under radar detection along the Atlantic coast until reaching the mainland from the Nova Scotia area into Maine. The pilot indicated he was carrying two passengers, Lawrence and Leonard Bean, owners of an apparel company in Maine.

As the aircraft landed, Singh appeared in his stolen vehicle. He parked the car and walked into the tiny terminal and peered out the glass windows facing the single runway. The Falcon was taxiing toward the terminal and, as it arrived, airport personnel were running toward the plane. Singh watched as the plane's door opened and Answa proceeded down the steps to the tarmac. Once there, Singh could see him talking to the officials and guiding them away from the plane back towards the terminal.

"Captain Kocon has remained on the plane to shut down all systems. He will then call the Falcon people who will arrive in a day or so to inspect the plane while my brother and I attend to some business in the Providence area. My brother Leonard is mute and needs to re-attach his hearing aids before he leaves the plane. He cannot fly with them on, they block his ears badly." Answa's English was perfect, having studied at Eton University in England years before. The officials were not overly trained in emergency procedures since they seldom had any to worry about at this small air strip. They were impressed with Answa's friendliness and candor and offered to help in any way they could. It was ironic that the officials never suspected that the Beans were of Arabic descent, even though their darker skin and British accent were not exactly indicative of people from Bangor.

Answa and his henchman posing as his mute brother entered the terminal and were greeted by Singh. The pilot had been instructed to go through the routine for engine trouble by pretending to do a series of checks at the controls of the aircraft and had been threatened by Answa that his wife in Khatamori would be killed if he revealed where they really came from. Kocon was to await a phone call from Answa in two days and, in the meantime, was to check in at the Radisson Hotel adjacent to the airport. Answa could be very persuasive. Singh briefed Answa on what had transpired and flashed a copy of the Saturday edition of the Boston Globe which reported the apparent success of the kidney transplant on Ahmad the day before. All three men boarded the stolen vehicle and headed for Singh's apartment just off Route 495 in Medway. The drive took about thirty minutes and was mostly in silence except for occasional questions from Answa who was pleased at Singh's new appearance.

"Our primary target will now have to be Ahmad, and if we succeed there, we will take care of Mr. Elliott after that. Once that is over, no one can stop me from the crown in Khatamori. No one!" muttered Answa. "We must find a way to get into the hospital undetected. Ahmad will be highly medicated and sometimes the reaction to medication can be deadly," he said with a sneer. "I have a plan for us and we will discuss this over dinner tonight. Fajid, you have disposed of Abou?" he continued.

"Yes, that has been taken care of and it may be quite some time before the police realize that only one of us remains. With my new look and name, no one will suspect anything."

CHAPTER 22

Answa entered the small apartment that Singh had rented and prepared to execute his plan to assassinate Ahmad at Mass. General. He retrieved a suitcase that his henchman carried and proceeded to the bathroom. After opening and placing the suitcase on the floor near the sink, Answa began to create his disguise. He reached for a beard and began to place it on his face. When it looked perfect, he reached for a pair of rimless glasses and put them on. Next he reached for a turban and carefully put it on. When he was convinced that the disguise looked genuine, he went into the suitcase again and pulled out a Polaroid camera. He stood against a plain solid wall and asked Singh to take his picture, making sure that the picture did not go below his chest. Singh took several of these to be sure at least one came out to Answa's satisfaction.

Once an adequate photo was chosen, Answa cropped the photo and inserted it with paper glue inside the passport he had with him. The name on the passport was Sanji Mubarrah from Khatamori. There, in fact, was a real Sanji Mubarrah and he was the spiritual leader for Muslims in Khatamori. Mubarrah, however, was still in Khatamori and leading its people in general prayer services for the well-being of King Ahmad. Answa even had the Muslim spiritual robe to make his disguise complete. If he couldn't get into the hospital to see Ahmad with these credentials, no one could.

Late Friday evening, he had Singh drive him to the Copley Hotel in Boston where he registered for a room under Mubarrah's name. He then told Singh and his henchman to steal another car and head back to Medway with their own phony credentials. If their plans succeeded, they would meet on Sunday at another hotel, The Belmont Hotel on Boylston St. If either did not show up at the Belmont, the other would know that one had failed, either in killing Ahmad or Bob Elliott.

On Saturday morning, Answa headed by taxi for Mass. General carrying a concealed gun with a silencer attached under his robe, pleased with the result of his disguise and carrying his fake passport for identification. The day was cool, but sunny, as his taxi pulled up to the main entrance of Mass. General. He immediately proceeded to the Visitors' Desk and asked where the chapel was.

"Third floor, down the hall on the left, you can't miss it," the receptionist blurted without so much as looking up.

Answa boarded the elevator and headed up to the third floor, making sure that he did not attract too much attention, even though his garb would have appeared out of the ordinary in this Boston surrounding. As he arrived and entered the dimly lit small chapel, he could not help but notice a tall and large-shouldered clergyman kneeling in a pew at the front, near a small altar affixed with a crucifix in the center. The chapel was simple but provided quiet solitude for family members in need of an area to pray for their loved ones following surgery or struggling with some debilitating or life-threatening procedure.

Answa entered a pew at the rear of the chapel and tried to size up the large man up front. He proceeded to that area and tapped the man on his shoulder.

"Excuse me, Father, are you the hospital chaplain," he muttered in somewhat of a British accent.

"No, I'm not, my name is Father Merrill, but Father O'Malley, the one you're looking for, should be here in just a few minutes," responded Father Dick, at first not giving this religiously clad figure much attention.

"Father O'Malley, you say, thank you, I need to introduce myself to him as I have come a long way to pray for my king and to ask him to assist me as I visit him later on."

Father Dick focused on the Arab and asked, "By your king, you are not by any chance referring to King Ahmad from Khatamori are you?"

"Why, yes, of course. I am Sanji Mubarrah, the Imam of Khatamori and the king's personal spiritual counselor. I have just arrived from our country to pray over my king and to bring all the good wishes from the people of his kingdom."

Suspiciously, Father Dick followed, "and the queen, she is here as well?"

"Oh, yes, Queen Farah will be by his side almost day and night I believe. They are nearly inseparable."

"She was here in the chapel just about fifteen minutes ago, a very petite woman, I thought."

"Oh, no, Father, you must be mistaken, Queen Farah is quite tall and not of Arabian descent, she originally comes from France and does not have the darker skin like most Khatamori women."

"I see, I guess I really did not get a close enough look at her, it's pretty dark in here, but this woman was dressed in a robe and I assumed it was her," Father Dick went on as he eyed Answa very carefully now.

Before Father Dick could question Answa further, Father O'Malley appeared and walked directly toward Father Dick.

"Father Merrill, are we ready to go down to see the king now?" he chimed.

"Uh, very soon, Father, but this is the king's spiritual leader who's just arrived and would like to join us, is that possible?"

"Surely it's possible, Father Merrill, but with all the security down there, how do we know that this man is who he says he is. No offense, your holiness."

"The king does not have many enemies, I can assure you, and here is my passport to substantiate my identity, Father O'Malley," Answa responded.

O'Malley glanced at the passport photo inside and seemed convinced of its authenticity. Father Dick was not so convinced. Why hadn't Françoise mentioned him before, perhaps because she still was a Catholic and not close to Mubarrah or the Muslim faith, or that she simply was too preoccupied to remember that Mubarrah was coming. Nevertheless, Father Dick was not about to take chances. He excused himself to go to the bathroom before they headed to the recovery area, knowing that Father O'Malley would wait for him to return before heading down to the recovery area.

Once out of the chapel, Father Dick headed straight for the nurse's station near the elevator and asked for the telephone number in the exclusive restricted area where Françoise was resting. As the phone rang, Father Dick felt bad about disturbing her but wanted to run Mubarrah by her.

Françoise answered groggily, obviously having awakened from a much needed sleep following a few days of restlessness.

"Richard, what is it?" Françoise shouted.

"Françoise, there is a holy man here who says he is Ahmad's spiritual counselor in Khatamori, his name is Sanji Mubarrah. He wants to see Ahmad to pray over him but I wanted to make sure who he was first."

"Yes, Richard, Sanji is Ahmad's friend and counselor. Does this man wear a turban and does he have a long beard?"

"Yes, he does, I'm sorry to have awakened you. Get some rest."

CHAPTER 23

Harry, in the Providence FBI office, began checking any non-commercial flights landing at any airport in Massachusetts or Rhode Island. One of the agents assisting Harry noticed the arrival of a Falcon jet at North Central Airport in Lincoln. The agent followed up on the plane's identification number and attempted to match it to Maine records, the location the plane had arrived from. There were no records of two brothers owning the aircraft. The agent called the business in question and one of the brothers picked up the phone. He explained to the agent how his brother had died two years earlier of leukemia. He further explained that the company no longer owned a plane and certainly never owned a Falcon jet.

Harry arrived at the small airport in Lincoln at 10:00 a.m. and, with another agent already there waiting for his arrival, proceeded toward the Falcon jet parked near a hangar at the far end of the terminal area. The staircase to the plane led to a partially open doorway as they approached, guns drawn. Harry and the other agent cautiously ascended the stairs and burst into the plane. The noise startled the pilot who was sprawled out on a sofa at the rear of the plane.

"Is anyone else in here," Harry shouted.

The pilot shook his head.

The two men carefully proceeded toward the pilot with the second agent looking behind them as Harry neared the pilot. Harry ripped off the tape and asked, "Who are you and why are you here?"

"My name is Captain Ed Kocon and I am the private pilot for King Ahmad Maurier of Khatamori. I was held at gunpoint by the king's cousin, Answa Talon, and instructed to fly here yesterday. They said they had my wife back in Khatamori and if I didn't do exactly as they said, they would kill her and then me. What else could I do?"

"Let me see your passport."

Kocon reached for his jacket's inside pocket and, sure enough, the passport appeared legitimate and American issue.

"Where is Talon?" Harry asked.

"I don't know. He and his bodyguard met another man at the terminal and left about twelve hours ago."

Harry raced to his car and picked up his car phone and told the dispatcher to put him through to the agents stationed at Mass. General.

"We're now looking for three men, possibly four, and we have evidence that they landed here in Rhode Island sometime yesterday. Have someone go to the king's suite back at the Westin and see if they have or can get us a photo of this Answa Talon, the king's cousin. We have reason to believe he may attempt to get to the king at Mass. General." The agent said he would get right on it.

Harry responded by letting the agent know that he was leaving for Mass. General and would be there in less than an hour. He then told the agent back in the plane to have other agents on hand in and around the Falcon jet in the event that Talon and his men returned there.

Harry's Ford Fairlane headed up Route 95 toward Boston at speeds exceeding eighty miles per hour and he had his flashing lights going without the siren turned on. He was always amazed at how motorists rapidly got out of your way when they saw flashing lights in the rear view mirror. He was sure that many of them were thinking that the flashing lights were meant for them as they exceeded the allowed speed limit on the highway.

He grabbed his car phone again and this time asked the operator to connect him with field agents at Mass. General.

"This is Agent Harry Esten and I need to speak to one of the FBI agents watching King Ahmad's recovery area."

Agent Hannaway answered, "Hannaway, how can I help you Harry?"

"Has anyone tried to visit the king today, other than the queen and Father Merrill?"

"Only the hospital chaplain who stopped by earlier, why?"

"Call me if anyone else comes within fifty feet of that area. I should be there in less than an hour."

Answa and Father O'Malley were glad to see Father Dick return and they were ready to head down to the recovery area. As they left the chapel, Answa couldn't help but notice the "Out of Service" sign posted on the front of the elevator. It instructed users to use the elevator at the far end of that floor instead. Father O'Malley was upset at seeing this sign as his walk was slow, the result of a bad knee he had incurred in a fall some years earlier. He knew all too well that the far end meant halfway around the floor, completely at the opposite side of where the chapel was located. As they began to proceed toward that direction, Father Dick noticed the anxiety in Talon's face and the perspiration that appeared on his brow. Talon knew that the journey to the king's room would take longer now that Father O'Malley slowed the pace significantly.

Killing Ahmad would take a little while longer.

CHAPTER 24

Singh and the henchman, dressed in business suits, arrived at 10:00 a.m. in an unmarked car at the Elliott residence in Medway where they were stopped by the Medway police. Singh and his accomplice flashed a badge indicating that they were from Interpol and that they had been on the trail of Singh and DeSai following several murders in Europe of eastern dignitaries attending oil conferences in Rome. After checking flights out of Rome, the men tracked the two assassins to a flight to Boston. After telling the local police on duty outside the Elliott house that the FBI had instructed them about the threat on Bob Elliott, the two Interpol agents thought that they could be of service if their capture warranted interrogation in their native tongue. The Medway police bought the story and their credentials and allowed them to stick around.

"I repeat, we're now looking for at least three people, maybe four. Have Kaleel, the king's assistant, fax you a photo of Talon. Give him the hospital fax number," Harry repeated.

"Hold on, Harry, looks like the chaplain is coming back this way with that Father Merrill and another spiritual guy in a turban and robes."

"Anyone check the credentials of this other guy?" The silence on the other end of the phone line was deafening as the agent searched for what to say since he had not personally done so.

"I'll do it now, Harry, before he's allowed in the room." As the agent put the phone down, Harry shouted into the telephone, "Do not let anyone within fifty feet of that room. Hello, hello?"

Harry was just minutes away from Mass. General and he found himself beginning to sweat profusely as he veered his car in and out of Boston traffic until the hospital was in sight. He pulled up in front of the main doors and began running down the corridor to the elevators to the second floor recovery area. The local policemen on duty were oblivious of any imminent danger as Harry charged past them, badge flashing as he raced by.

As he approached the recovery area, the other agent he had just spoken to noticed him coming.

"Where are they, the clergy that was here a few minutes ago," Harry blurted.

"I checked the passport of the Arab guy and he's ok, Harry."

Harry burst into Ahmad's room and confronted the three men. He immediately headed directly toward Talon and asked to see his identification again. The disguised

Talon, insulted at this crass approach, shoved Harry down and bolted from the room.

As he hurried down the hall, he yelled to the agent and local police, "There's trouble in the room, please hurry, one of the men is on the floor."

The police instinct was to rush toward the room, almost ignoring Talon as he kept on walking past them.

Father Dick helped Harry up, slightly shaken, but fully aware that this man who just bolted out of the room was surely no holy man.

As the police and the agent entered the room, Harry shouted, "Block all the exits, alert the men to be on their toes for anyone trying to leave the hospital, anyone."

Two uniformed Boston policemen assumed their guard outside Ahmad's room while Father Dick and Father O'Malley were still in shock at what had just happened.

"No one enters this room, no one, until I say so." Harry barked.

The other FBI agent was on his walkie-talkie instructing all men to block all exits as the manhunt began for Talon. Talon headed for a staircase and ran down to the lower floor of the hospital, the area where emergency vehicles arrived. As he ran, he also removed his disguise. First, the robe which was difficult to run with, then the turban and beard, tossing these into a hospital laundry cart near the entry door to the emergency area. Spotting a door marked Employees Only, Talon entered and found himself in a locker room. Grabbing a white lab coat, a clipboard, and a stethoscope hanging on an open locker room door, he exited and headed toward a door leading to a ramp near the ambulance area.

Harry reached the lower floor and spotted Talon at the end of the hallway and yelled for him to stop. Talon turned and fired at Harry, hitting him in the shoulder. Harry staggered but kept his balance and drew his own gun and, before he could return the fire, Talon was out the door. Talon raced down into the hospital's laundry area, adjacent to another staircase leading to the parking garage where laundry delivery trucks loaded and unloaded linen for the hospital. As he raced outside, Talon fired at a driver who immediately abandoned his truck and ran for cover. Talon jumped into the van and sped toward the exit to the garage. Harry bolted from the doorway, one arm hanging from the recent gunshot, and fired directly at Talon through the windshield of the vehicle, striking Talon in the head and causing the van to crash against a cement wall, bursting into flames. Within a moment, Harry collapsed to the ground as other police arrived. Hospital attendants nearby quickly placed Harry on a gurney and emergency assistants attempted to apply pressure to Harry's wound. Luckily, the bullet had entered and exited without hitting a bone or major artery.

Two hours later, Harry was discharged from the hospital, his left arm comforted by a sling. Before leaving, he placed a call to Chief Anderson in Medway to tell him about Talon's death but that others were still at large.

Anderson informed Harry that the rental car they had been looking for had been found in a parking lot with the body of what appeared to be an Arab in the trunk of the vehicle.

"That leaves two at large, what's going on at your end?" Harry inquired.

"Nothing much, just two Interpol guys who were also on the Arabs trail from Europe where these guys are suspected in other murders."

"I should be in Medway tomorrow morning, Chief, but for now I think I'd better take the night off," Harry moaned. "You've got my car phone number and you can also reach me at my home number in Providence."

CHAPTER 25

Harry, having been discharged from Mass. General, got a lift from another agent who agreed to drive his car for him back to Providence. Before leaving, however, he made a visit to Queen Farah to inform her that Talon had been killed in a failed attempt to get to the king. The queen was extremely thankful to Harry and she uncontrollably hugged him for what felt like an eternity to Harry, not to mention the pain it brought to his wounded arm. She would tell the king immediately upon his awakening which was expected later during the day and she expressed to Harry how the king himself would want to thank him personally at some later date. Harry quickly pointed out that there were still two other assassins still not found and that the king was not out of danger yet. Security in and around the king's hospital room would be increased for as long as necessary.

Father Dick also expressed his thanks to Harry as he was accompanying Françoise to Ahmad's room. Father O'Malley was still stunned at what had just transpired.

If the other two assassins were targeting Ahmad and not Bob Elliott, Harry realized that the danger to Ahmad was far from over.

Harry arrived home at five in the afternoon and was looking forward to unwinding as he made himself a dry Southern Comfort Manhattan and, as he kicked off his shoes and undid his bloodied necktie, he picked up the phone and called Jim Howard to let him know what had happened. Jim offered to stop in for a visit, but Harry was suddenly feeling the effects of his wound and the painkillers that the hospital had administered and felt in no mood for visitors. Howard understood and said he would catch up with Harry in a day or so.

As he let himself get totally relaxed as he sipped his drink ever so slowly, Harry suddenly jumped up, as if an alarm had just gone off.

"Interpol, how does Interpol know that the two assassins are in Medway?"

Harry raced to the phone and dialed the Providence office.

"This is Harry Esten—put me through to the Interpol office in Germany. This is very important."

In what appeared to be ten minutes of silence on the other end of the receiver, but in fact was less than a minute, a voice in a German accent answered on the other end.

"Interpol, how may I direct your call?"

"My name is Harry Esten, FBI badge number three-two-six-seven from Providence, Rhode Island, in the United States and I must speak to whoever's in charge, please."

Within seconds, Gerhard Schmidt came on the line and inquired how he could be of service.

"You have two agents now in the US in pursuit of Fajid Singh and Abou Ben Habib, also known as Muhammad DeSai." Harry carefully pronounced the names as best he could. He then told Schmidt the names of the two Interpol agents in Medway.

Schmidt was puzzled. "We don't have any agents in the US. Our agents travel mostly throughout Europe and seldom leave the continent and we don't have agents by those names anyway."

Harry hung up the phone, waited a few seconds, then picked up the receiver to get a dial tone. He tried to enter the Medway police telephone so fast that he fumbled it a few times until finally hearing the ring at the other end. When he asked to speak to Chief Anderson, the operator indicated that he was not in.

"Pass me through to one of the squad cars at the Elliott house."

"Sergeant Turcotte, here."

"I need to speak to Chief Anderson, this is FBI agent Harry Esten, this is urgent."

"The Chief is heading up the walk to the Elliott house right now," Turcotte answered.

"Is anyone else with him?" Harry shouted.

"Yep, those two Interpol guys."

"Stop them now, now, do you hear me?"

"Chief, FBI agent Esten is on the line, says it's urgent."

Turning briefly to the two agents, Anderson shrugged. "Hold on, fellas, I've got to take this call."

Singh grabbed Anderson's shoulder and, as he did, Anderson could feel the barrel of a gun against his back.

"I don't think so, Chief. I think you want to be calm right now and tell your officer that you'll get back to the FBI in a couple of minutes. We have someone inside we need to meet first." Singh grabbed Anderson's gun from his holster as he spoke.

"What the hell, oh shit, you guys aren't Interpol are you?"

"Eddie, tell Agent Esten I'm busy on a two-four-six and I'll get back to him."

"Two-four-six, two-four-six, what's he saying, that's 'in pursuit of a suspect, armed and dangerous.'"

Sergeant Turcotte reacted immediately, drew his pistol and shielded himself behind his squad car as he shouted, "Stop right there assholes, all of you, and lay your weapons on the ground right now, do it now!"

Singh held Anderson in front of him with his gun now pointed to Anderson's head as they back peddled toward the Elliott front door. Bob Elliott heard the commotion outside as he was pouring a cup of coffee for Sergeant Miller, after Miller had delivered the mail a few minutes earlier. It dawned on Bob that no one had seen Miller enter the house as he had done so by the patio entrance in the rear of the house where another patrolman was stationed.

The knock on the door was followed by a weak shout from Anderson, "Bob, it's Chief Anderson, I have a few questions for you."

Bob rushed the rest of the family upstairs and told them to get into the bedroom and to lock the doors behind them as they entered. He tried not to sound alarmed but the look on his face gave it away. As the family rushed upstairs, Miller drew his gun and Bob told him to hide in the hallway closet until he could see what was happening.

"Come on in, Chief, the door's unlocked."

As the three entered the house, Singh still had his arm around Anderson and the henchman was right behind them.

Bob headed through the living room and into the dining room. Singh whacked Anderson over the head with the butt of his gun and fired a shot at Bob, narrowly missing him. As he ran after Bob, Miller jumped out from behind the closet door and pointed his gun directly at the henchman who was startled to see him appear out of nowhere. The henchman tried to fire at Miller, but Miller shot three times in his direction, hitting him twice in the chest as he fell to the floor. Singh spun around momentarily to see what had just happened and saw the henchman fall. He continued his pursuit toward the dining room which led to the kitchen area. As he rounded the corner from the living room to the dining room, he never knew what hit him. Bob Elliott laced a solid baseball bat to Singh's head, his gun going off skyward shooting wildly at the ceiling. Bob's next blow knocked the gun from Singh's hand and, as quick as a flash, Miller appeared pointing his gun at Singh as he kicked Singh's gun away from his body. Singh was holding his head which was bleeding profusely and Miller called outside for medical help from Sergeant Turcotte.

Within seconds, ambulances arrived and the house was swarming with police. Bob rushed upstairs once he realized that Singh's stray shots had gone through the ceiling where the bedrooms were located. Luckily, the family had locked themselves in a rear bedroom far away from the gunfire.

CHAPTER 26

There are always more visitors at hospitals on a Sunday, but the security outside Ahmad's room had now been lessened with the capture of the two remaining assailants. Françoise was by his side when Ahmad finally awoke from the sedation following the transplant surgery.

"Hello, my husband," Françoise gently spoke with a broad smile on her face, "I trust you slept well. Everything went well with the surgery and, in time, you also will be well again."

"I am happy to see you again, especially on this day rather than in the next life, my queen," Ahmad quietly responded as the two held each other's hands warmly.

"There is more good news. Your cousin Answa is dead and his associates have been captured and arrested by the F.B.I. when they tried to kill my son, Robert Elliott, in

Medway, Massachusetts late yesterday. The authorities are questioning Singh to make certain that there are no others seeking to kill you or Robert. I think the nightmare is over, Ahmad."

"You will not be at peace, Françoise, until you face this Robert Elliott and try to explain why you abandoned him so many years ago. A child has a right to know how a mother could do this to her sons. He must want to know you if you are ever to get over the guilt feeling you now have. I will always be there for you, and for your son also, but you must go to him, my love; you must do this now while we are here."

"Richard has told me that Robert was not happy to meet him and that we had no right to endanger his family. I fear that my visit to him will be no different but, as always my dear husband, you are correct, I must face my son."

At that moment, Father Dick entered the room and Ahmad immediately knew who he was, even though they had never met. Françoise was about to introduce him to Ahmad when Ahmad interjected, "and I take it that this is your long lost priest of many years ago?"

"Your Highness, I am Father Richard Merrill and I am very pleased to meet you. Françoise has told me so much about you."

"I wish I could say that Françoise has told me a great deal about you as well, Father Merrill, but, then again, she really does not know that much about you, does she?"

"That is quite true, Your Highness. A brief encounter thirty-six years ago doesn't say much about who I really am, does it?" he echoed.

"Françoise tells me that, without your help and the people you confided in, I might not have been here today.

That does tell me the kind of man you are and I thank you for that. We will talk more later, but for now, Françoise has somewhere she needs to be, and I am tired and need to rest more."

Father Dick understood perfectly and left the telephone number and address where he could be reached in Lincoln. Françoise led Father Dick out and she again thanked him for all his help as she hugged him tightly for several seconds.

It was sunny that afternoon as Father Dick got in his car and headed back to Rhode Island. For the first time in over a week, he felt some sense of relief that some of this burden had been lifted from his shoulders. He would, of course, arrange for a meeting with the bishop of the Providence diocese to explain the events leading to the development of his sudden fatherhood. The bishop's guidance on how to handle a priest's son was something he would need assistance with.

CHAPTER 27

The limousine pulled up to Tiffany Lane in Medway and a policeman stepped out of his cruiser to see who was parking in front of Bob Elliott's home. The driver got out of the limo, walked around the car, and opened the rear passenger door where Françoise stepped out. She was dressed in her formal regal attire and stood erect to greet the officer. Once she explained who she was and the purpose of her visit, the police officer walked up the front walk and rang the doorbell.

"Hi, Bob, you've got a visitor. A Queen Farah of Khatamori. She said you would know what it's about."

"Thanks, Stan; I do know what it's about. Have her come up, would you," Bob stated with a concerned look.

The fifty feet up that walk felt like Françoise's longest as she nervously approached the image before her. Her heart pounded and tears streamed down her cheek as she faced her son, the child she had abandoned because she did not know any better over thirty-five years earlier. If only she could turn back time and relive that moment at the orphanage when she relinquished her rights to both sons. It was because of her that Charles Larouche was dead and because of her that Bob Elliott had been in danger of losing his own life.

"Hello, I'm Bob, would you like to come inside?" Bob spoke as he extended his right hand in a warm greeting as he noticed the tears streaming down her face.

"I am Queen Farah from Khatamori and formerly Françoise Dupont from Paris, France and, most importantly, your birth mother who made a very stupid decision so many years ago."

"Please, come inside, you should meet the rest of my family and we can talk."

This was not the same Bob Elliott who had earlier been less than courteous to Father Dick. As the events of the weekend became clearer to him, and as he spoke with his parents about the adoption and the years of financial support that followed, Bob realized that Françoise had been wise enough back then to seek help from the orphanage, even though he still remained confused on having been abandoned. Carl and Judy, his adopted parents, also felt remorse for Françoise and the need for Bob to meet his natural parents, whatever the circumstances.

The greetings from Bob's parents were genuinely warm as they also were pleased to finally meet the very generous person who cared enough about her son to assure that he was financially secure in his adoptive surroundings throughout his youthful years. Françoise also seemed to hold a special feeling towards Carl and Judy as she expressed the gratitude toward them for raising such a fine son, a responsibility that should have been hers. Bob's wife, Julie, also greeted Françoise with a tender smile as she asked her to sit in the living room nearby. Ben found all of this quite fascinating.

"I want to thank you for allowing me into your home, Robert, it is something that I should have done years ago and, perhaps, your brother, Charles, would still be alive today and someone you should have known. I have never seen him myself and it is now God's will that we will only meet in Heaven. Please try not to judge me too quickly. I was alone, without much money, and desperate to do the right thing so many years ago in Paris. There was no way I could care for both of you and the orphanage was kind enough to help me when no one else could or would. When the years passed and I met my husband, Ahmad, I made sure that your parents had enough to raise you well. I did the same for Charles' parents even though I knew that this was only a way for me to hide behind my guilt in having abandoned you to begin with. I see now that you are all that a mother could ask for and I'm certain Charles was as well."

Françoise went on. "As a queen who has many loyal people who depend on her for guidance and help, I buried myself in my work to help the children in my country as my way to be the mother to them that I was not to you. I do not ask you to forgive me for what I have done, but that you understand what I did as a young, foolish woman who cannot erase that decision. Understand, Robert, that I have and will always love you as my son and that you are forever welcome in my home. Perhaps, at some other time, if you would want, we might talk again. My husband's enemies have either been captured or killed and you and your family should no longer be in danger. Ahmad's kidney operation went well and we will be leaving for Khatamori next Friday, if what the doctors say is true and I have no reason to doubt them. We will be at the Westin until then."

Françoise rose to say goodbye to the Elliott family and extended her hand to each of them in friendliness. When she confronted Bob again, there was no anger on his face or resentment toward this woman. There seemed to be compassion in his eyes as they met hers and, without speaking, he forgave her. As their hands met, Bob smiled and held her extended hand in both of his. Françoise's eyes began to water as she returned the smile.

She turned to them all and said, "You should not discuss this with anyone, and it would only create more questions and problems for you. But I repeat my open invitation to you to visit Khatamori in the future as our guests. It is very beautiful and we have a fragrance in the air that is warm and peaceful, you would like it."

"Goodbye to all of you and thank you for allowing me to meet you. I must now be with my husband."

As she headed for the front door, Bob stopped in her way and said, "Would you care for a cup of tea or coffee and stay a while longer before you head back to Boston?"

CHAPTER 28

Françoise stayed and chatted for another hour before she left for Boston in her limousine. She sensed so much relief at what had just transpired that she cried the entire trip back. Bob had not rejected her and a bridge had been built to further the relationship. As she entered Ahmad's hospital room and found him awake, he also could sense the relief in her eyes. The calmness in the room lasted for quite some time before Ahmad finally spoke.

"It went well with your son?"

"Yes, my love, it was much more than I expected or deserved."

"You are not an evil woman, Françoise, there is only so much suffering that anyone can bear. It will get better now."

Ahmad's treatment in Boston continued to improve his health and he would be allowed to leave for home on Friday as originally planned. In Khatamori, a specialist had been hired by Ahmad to attend to him over the next month while also bringing his expertise to the hospital in Banra.

Father Dick called Jim Howard and thanked him for all of his help in the events of the previous week. He mentioned that Jack Bumpus obviously knew his men well and Jim had certainly been the right choice to assist him.

In Medway, the doorbell rang at Bob Elliott's home and Julie answered. Standing in the doorway was a very distinguished Arab with a package for her and Robert. As Julie quickly opened the package, she uncovered a mahogany box adorned with jewels. Inside the box, there lay a large gold-plated bottle with a note attached. Julie clumsily opened the note which read:

Smell the fragrance of Khatamori, the Flower of Heaven.

Françoise and Ahmad